Lost

In

Love

darrell denham

Fulton Books
Meadville, PA

Published by Fulton Books 2022

ISBN 978-1-63860-688-8 (paperback)
ISBN 979-8-88505-917-6 (hardcover)
ISBN 978-1-63860-687-1 (digital)

Printed in the United States of America

To my wife, Sue McMillan Denham, thank
you for being so encouraging and patient.
I am a better person because of you.

Acknowledgments

There are two people I will forever be indebted to for helping me realize the dream I have long had of writing a novel—Sue Denham and Vickie Ashley.

First, there is my wife, Sue, who is my chief critic, editor, and ear for my thoughts. Her objective criticism and suggestions are responsible for adding depth and polish to this work.

Second, there is Vickie Ashley. Aside from reading the work and offering her input, she has a rare ability to transform my scrawl into a legible typed document. The effort she made in choosing the different nuances used to make the novel a better read told me I had chosen the right person for the job.

I want to thank Melissa Easterday for her invaluable assistance in helping me give the Scottish characters in the novel an authentic voice.

I would also like to thank several ladies who read my novel and gave me the encouragement to continue this journey: Jean Courson, Vivian Manley, Paula Norris, Margaret Phelps, and Gina Devin.

Finally, I would like to thank all the people associated with Fulton Books for their effort in making this dream a reality.

Can someone truly be the love of your life if you only share ten days together? That's a rhetorical question, for Caitie still comes to me in moments of solitude. And my thoughts drift back to those days—those days so long ago and what might have been. I still hold you so dear, my love.

M. W.

PART 1

Betrayal and Redemption

Chapter One

Edinburgh, 2004

aitlin blinked her eyes and squinted to allow time for them to adjust to the harsh light. Tears welled in the corner of her eyes as the pain, which had been suppressed by the adrenaline, moved through her body. *What happened to me, and where am I?*

Caitlin focused enough to see a young woman dressed in white, writing on a clipboard at her bedside. *I am in hospital, but why?*

"It's good to see you have joined us," the young nurse noted as she looked down at her.

"What happened?"

"The paramedics who responded to the call said you took a tumble off your bike. Do you recall anything?"

"I remember riding my bike, then my foot slipped off the pedal. I felt strange, and everything went black."

"You were lucky. The man who called 999 said you just veered off the path and fell over."

"My wrist," Caitlin said as she slowly twisted it.

"Let's try not to move it unless necessary until the doctor does his assessment. I need to get some basic information if you feel up to it."

"Sure."

"Name?"

"Caitlin Campbell."

"Age?"

"Thirty-one."

A tall man dressed in scrubs pushed through the curtain surrounding the bed Caitlin was in and closed it behind him. "I see we have another success story for the NHS," he quipped as he smiled.

"Dr. Morrison, you should know better," the nurse chided.

"Yes, Nurse Wilson, I should. Yet it is hard to resist. Just an inside joke that I should save for the pub. Now who do we have here as our patient?"

"I haven't done the full profile yet sir, but her name is Caitlin Campbell."

"Well, Ms. Campbell, it is a pleasure to meet you," Ian said while he admired the beautiful red hair that framed Caitlin's face as she lay in the bed.

"I wish I could say the same."

"Touché. We do have a live one, Jenny. Have we assessed the particulars of her misfortune?"

"No, Doctor, I was—"

"That's fine," Ian interrupted. Turning his attention to the patient, he was drawn to her eyes, those bright green eyes that seemed to shimmer in the harsh light. "Let's do turn the lights down." Moving beside her bed, Ian took a closer look at her eyes and noted there were no abnormalities. "I need to check your pulse and listen to your heart."

"My right wrist hurts."

"Fortunately, we come with two," Ian said as he took Caitlin's left wrist and checked her pulse. Satisfied, he took his stethoscope and listened to her heart. "Good pulse and good heart rate. So, Ms. Campbell, can you tell me where the pain is located?"

"My wrist and head hurt, and my shoulder but not as much as my head or wrist."

Ian took a close look at the area on the right side of Caitlin's forehead. It had been cleaned, so there was little worry concerning infection. But the visible swelling indicated she had suffered a significant blow. "I fear you are going to have quite a bit of bruising."

"I guess I'll just tell everyone I ran into a door."

"So you are married."

"No."

"My apology for assuming," Ian said as he turned his attention to Caitlin's wrist. Ian gently held the injured wrist and gingerly probed for any abnormalities. When he finished, he did the same in the shoulder area. "Hopefully, there are no breaks, but we will know more after we take a few pictures."

"Okay."

"Do you have any pain in your legs or back? There are some abrasions on your knee."

"No, I feel fine other than my head and wrist."

"I see from the notes Nurse Wilson recorded that you said your foot slipped."

"Yes."

"Have you had any trouble lately with similar instances, slipping or falling?"

"Not really."

"Also, the report says everything went black?"

"Yes."

"Was this prior to your foot slipping?"

"Not sure."

"Any other episodes of blacking out?"

"No."

"Okay, Ms. Campbell, I want you to relax for a few minutes while I request a few x-rays."

"Is it necessary? I feel fine now. I could just call someone to pick me up."

"No. No. We have a special today. Three x-rays for the price of one, and I insist."

Caitlin looked puzzled. "I don't understand."

"I apologize. Nurse Wilson often reminds me that my attempts at humor should be given in small doses, Ms. Campbell. I think it would be proper if we took a few x-rays to err on the side of caution, as they say. Hopefully, we will find everything is normal, and all that will be required is a brace or cast for you to exit our esteemed institution."

"Okay."

"Great. Now I need to make the necessary arrangements, but first, I must speak with Nurse Wilson concerning another matter. So if you will excuse us, it'll only take a moment."

"Sure, but I need to call my mum."

"Yes, she will take care of that in a few minutes," Ian said as he walked through the curtain, followed by Nurse Wilson. He then closed the curtain back before moving a short distance away, where he was confident the sounds of the A&E would muffle their conversation.

"Jenny, no further medications other than paracetamol for the present time, and make sure Ms. Campbell stays alert. Hopefully, I will be able to expedite the x-rays."

"What are your concerns?"

"It could be several things. The blacking out is troubling. She is young and in good physical condition, so I want to be sure she hasn't suffered a skull fracture or worse."

"Oh my, I'll be sure the other nurses know to check on her frequently."

"Thanks, Jenny. Now I have to go work my magic with Hakim."

"Good luck."

Ian smiled and walked to his workstation to put in the request for the x-rays. Since he was requesting several x-rays more than usual, he knew an explanation was required. He finished and then stared at the critical entry before he hit send.

Chapter Two

Ian was reviewing the records of the patients he had seen the past four hours as he waited for a few lab results and x-rays he had requested. As he glanced up, he saw Hakim walking in his direction. A slight smile from Hakim told Ian all was not well.

"Hakim, how has your day been?"

"Exhaustive. Can we speak in private, Dr. Morrison?"

"Of course, Dr. Patel," Ian said as he stood and walked out from behind the desk. Hakim then followed as Ian led the way. Ian stopped at a room marked Storage and stepped inside. Hakim followed him in and closed the door.

"Why so formal?" Ian asked.

"I don't wish for our colleagues to think our friendship has its benefits."

"Hakim, I don't think any would make such an assumption."

"Then why request my approval for tests that do not seem justified?"

"Hakim, I feel they are."

"Ian, we both know there are times when you make a request based more on intuition rather than following standard protocol."

Ian could tell Hakim was upset, and he knew he had put his friend in a difficult position. But his primary concern was to serve as an advocate for the patient. "Okay, just what would you have me do? Ignore something that could result in a possible health crisis?"

"Simply follow protocol, Ian. Honor the queue."

"Damn, Hakim, we are talking about patients' lives."

"I am aware. Here are the x-rays you requested for Caitlin Campbell. Your intuition was right this time. You need to schedule her for a biopsy."

"Thanks, Hakim. I appreciate this, and I'll try to work on the other." Ian started to leave, but Hakim was still standing in front of the door and had not moved. "Is there something else?"

"I was told by my immediate supervisor that I should start documenting such instances. Administration wishes to construct a profile for each physician at hospital, and you know how that can be used."

"Yes."

"Please keep that in mind, Ian."

"Thanks again, Hakim, and I apologize if I have put you in an awkward position."

Hakim nodded and left. Ian quickly flipped through the report. He was concerned about possible swelling, but the white mass he saw in the right frontal lobe area was not swelling. Caitlin Campbell had a tumor, and time was critical. *So young*, he thought as he closed the chart.

Chapter Three

Roseville, One week earlier

I stared through the dormer windows into an overcast sky, and my eyes gradually settled on the two oaks in the distance framing the entrance to Twin Oaks. How many times had I been told the story of how my parents planted those two trees to serve as a reminder that Twin Oaks will stand the test of time just as those majestic oaks?

"Michael, quit daydreaming! Remember we're on a quest!" Becky shouted across the attic.

Startled back into reality, I turned and saw my sister glaring at me. "Yes, Mother. I know. Focus on the job."

"Hey, you agreed to help me look for the angel. I didn't force you, so let's get on with the job."

I flashed a smile. "Okay, Becky. Just kidding," I said as I turned and pretended to be busy moving boxes in search of the elusive angel until I heard Becky resume her search. I then turned back to look at my sister.

To a six-year-old boy who understood little concerning what was appropriate and what wasn't, my thirteen-year-old sister had been my first love. She was this wondrous beauty who catered to my whims that ranged from playing the princess I had to rescue to climbing trees with me to escape the murderous pirates. She never seemed to tire of my wild imaginings. Strange, I never told Becky that I once had a crush on her as almost every boy in the county did at that time.

I often thought of the pain she had suffered. She married at nineteen, had two children before she was twenty-three, and divorced at twenty-six. I marveled at the strength she had shown in leaving an abusive husband. She laughed it off when she talked about it later, saying, "I ran out of excuses for the bruises, so I thought it was time." Becky later admitted to Mom that she realized the marriage was over when she made the decision to shoot Darien the next time he hit her.

I vividly recalled that day. Becky called Mom early in the morning, and after they talked, Mom came to my room. I could tell from the troubled expression on her face that something was terribly wrong. She told me Becky was leaving Darien, and she was on her way over with the kids. Mom then asked me if she needed to call Cliff. I realized at that moment I was officially being recognized as an adult. Dad was on a business trip, and Mom was concerned Darien might come to our house when he discovered Becky and the kids were gone. Mom was asking me to stand with her if there was a confrontation. I told her she didn't need to call Cliff, and it had worked out fine. Becky was finally able to escape the hell she had lived in for seven years.

Looking across the attic at Becky, I thought what a fool Darien was to squander his chance to share a life with such a beautiful princess. I continued to watch her for a few moments before resuming the search.

I carefully removed the lid from a large box to keep from scattering the dust and found it contained cards, letters, and several smaller boxes. Promising, I thought, but as I removed the lid from one of the small boxes, I saw it just contained more letters. I took the letter on top and read the name *Caitlin Campbell*. I was about to return it but stopped. How could this be? I did not understand. It had been fifteen years. I stared at the postmark on the letter, which read 1989. I poured the remaining letters into my hand and counted them. There were five letters, but I had only received one from Caitlin. It made no sense. Why would she continue to write? Caitlin had made it clear we were through. I slipped the letter with no envelope into my pocket, thinking I would read it later in private, and then returned the four remaining letters to the box.

Chapter Four

As I look back, the most amazing thing was that I had not exploded in anger, gone downstairs, and told my mother what I thought about her keeping the letters from me. Instead, Becky finally conceded the search for the missing angel tree topper was a quest that we would resume another day. So I simply went downstairs with Becky and acted as if I had never seen the letters.

I was sure Mom needed a break from entertaining Christy and the girls, so I told Christy I was ready to go. Twenty minutes later, we were home, and I put the letter in my desk before taking a shower.

I waited until Christy and the girls were in bed. It had been fifteen years, so I didn't think there was a need for any rush. I told Christy I needed to look over something for work and assured her I would not be long. I noted earlier the letter was only a single sheet of paper, so I felt certain I would be able to rejoin Christy in a few minutes. I kissed her and said, "I'll be back soon," and went downstairs to my office. I could not understand why there were more letters. Caitlin had made it clear we were done.

I pulled the desk drawer open, picked up the notebook I had placed over the letter, and took it out. After a deep breath, I carefully unfolded it and began to read.

Dearest Michael,

I received your letter a few days ago. For weeks, I had religiously checked the post each day with the hope I would finally hear from you, my love. "Be careful what you wish for" came to mind as I read your letter.

I am embarrassed when I think of all that I have shared with you in the earlier letters, and I struggle to understand how you could have changed so, but I know I must accept it. As per your request, I will make this my last letter, but I thought I would share something with you before I go. Today, our child moved, and it confirmed in me the belief that life is so very precious.

Love,
Caitlin

I could not take my eyes off that last line. How could they not tell me? I thought about riding to Twin Oaks and yelling at Mom. What gave her the right to keep this from me? It was my life! Then I thought of something. I took the only letter I thought Caitlin wrote me out of my wallet and laid it beside the other.

As soon as I saw them beside each other, it was obvious. The letter I had carried in my wallet the past fourteen years was a fake. In the fake letter, you could see the writer had looked at a sample of Caitlin's handwriting and made a good attempt to copy it. However, instead of being crisp and smooth like the letter I found in the attic, the handwriting in the fake letter was cumbersome and mechanical. There were numerous places where you could see the writer had stopped and then started again, trying to get it right. The contrast between the two letters was stark.

I wanted to kick myself. I should have taken all the letters, but I knew why I had not. No one noticed the one letter in my pocket, but it would have been obvious had I tried to take all five. As I continued to stare at the letters and the envelope, I realized how they had pulled off the deception.

It was an old trick—pair something legitimate with a good fake and it makes the deception harder to see. They had opened one of the letters Caitlin sent me, put the fake letter in the envelope, and resealed it. I saw what they wanted me to see—a letter from someone I loved. It also explained why the letter I took from the attic had no envelope. Stupid.

Stupid was all I could think as I continued to stare at the two letters.

I should have checked. I had samples of her handwriting. She had written several notes to me before that last day. I wanted to go to Twin Oaks, walk to my room, and look at the notes that were still in my freshman planner, but I knew it was useless. What would it change?

As I was staring at the letter, a thought came to me. *I may have a fourteen-year-old child I have never seen.*

Fifteen years. For fifteen years, my family had allowed me to live with this lie they concocted. Caitlin was most likely married, and I was a distant, unpleasant memory. Judging by the content of the letter, I was certain Caitlin had been a victim of the same sleight of hand. The two letters I sent to Caitlin were most likely intercepted, and one of the envelopes was used to fool Caitlin in the same manner they fooled me.

That was when I decided. Yes, I had a wife and two girls I loved dearly, but what my family did was insane. It altered the course of not only my life but also Caitlin's and our child's life. I would go to Scotland, apologize to Caitlin, and try to see my child.

I started thinking about how I might be able to make the trip and soon realized it would be best not to say anything to Mom or Christy. How would I tell them I needed to go see a girl I got pregnant when I was fifteen? I could imagine their reaction to such a request. It would not be pretty, and even if they eventually agreed, I would not have been in the frame of mind needed for a meeting with Caitlin and my child. I was sure it would be easier to get their forgiveness than secure their permission to go.

I then turned to the obvious question: How was I going to explain my absence for several days? That was going to be difficult, but I recalled something my cousin Cliff mentioned a few days ago and realized it just might work.

Chapter Five

I had been in the law office of Reinhardt and Carson for fifteen minutes. Tom Carson had taken care of the family's legal business for over twenty years, and I was almost certain he could provide me with the answers I needed. I knew there was a possibility he might refuse, but Tom and I had become close friends in the past few years. My hope was our friendship would tip the balance in my favor.

I looked up when I heard the door to his office open and saw Tom standing in the doorway, motioning for me to come in. He waited until I had walked into his office and closed the door before he spoke, "Are we still on for that round of golf Saturday morning?"

"Looking forward to it, Tom, but I need to step up my game some. That last round we played was brutal."

"It all depends on your perspective, Michael."

"Yeah, well, I guess you would say it was a good day, but then you didn't spend half of your round in a sand trap or the rough."

"Every dog has his day."

"I think this dog is still in search of that day, Tom."

"It will come, Michael. I think you are fairly good considering the amount of time you play. So what can I do for you today?"

"Tom, I am not sure of all the specifics concerning lawyer/client privilege, but I just need to be sure that what we talk about stays between us."

"Okay, I think I can assure you that will be the case."

"Including Mom."

"Understood."

"Tom, I know you probably can't tell me any particulars concerning the times you acted as a legal consultant for my mom and dad, even though it may have impacted me."

"That is correct. It would most likely violate their attorney/client privilege rights. Michael, I think it would be simpler if you were to just ask the questions you have, and I will answer them if I am able to."

So I asked, "What is Caitlin Campbell's address, and where does she work?"

"Now, see. That's better."

"Can you tell me?"

"Michael, as you suggested earlier, it would be best if I didn't discuss any previous dealings I may have been engaged in, involving this young lady and your parents. I can, however, procure information for a client. So yes, I believe I will be able to give you the answers to your questions. Would it be okay if I give this information to you Saturday morning?"

"That's fine. Do you—"

Tom interrupted, "Michael, before you say anything else, I was going to say the less I know, the better it is. Knowing your mom as I do, I definitely want to be out of the loop on this one."

"Sure. Mom always said you were good."

"Michael, there is good, and there is good. I am no saint, but there are days when I have to drink a little more than I should to get past some of the shit I am asked to do."

"Thanks, Tom, and I hope what I am asking is not one of these times."

"No. This is just research for a client. You just try to bring your game, Saturday."

"I will try, and thanks, Tom."

Tom waited until I walked out and closed the door. He then called his secretary. "Jen, please bring me the Campbell file."

"Yes, sir."

A few minutes later, Jen brought the file into Tom's office and placed it on his desk.

"Thanks, Jen."

"No problem, and you told me to remind you of the meeting scheduled with Ms. Davis at three."

"Yes, I should be through with this in a few minutes, and when you return it, pull the Davis file and bring it to me."

"Is there something else, sir?"

"No, Jen. I know I don't say this often enough, but I do appreciate the contribution you are making to this firm."

"Thank you, sir, and I appreciate the opportunity you gave me to work with you. I have found the work very interesting."

After Jen walked out and closed the door, Tom took the file, opened it, and found the information he needed. He copied it onto a piece of paper that he put in an envelope. After writing Michael's name on the envelope, he sealed it and slipped it into the inside pocket of his coat.

Chapter Six

Cliff let me nap as he drove until we were a few miles from Tifton. We were making good time, and the light traffic I saw on I-75 as we crossed over it would make it possible to do even better for the next hundred miles.

"Michael, I am going to stop at a place and get a coffee and a ham biscuit. You want anything?"

I sat up and pushed the hat out of my eyes. "Sure, I'll take a ham and egg with a coffee."

"Will do."

Cliff used the drive-through, picked up the food, and then pulled into an adjacent parking lot so we could eat before we got on the interstate. As we ate, we watched an endless stream of customers order and pick up their food.

"You know, Cliff, I don't believe we are the only ones that think this place has good food."

"Yeah, your dad would always stop here on the way north if he had the time. I keep meaning to go in one day and ask how it got its name."

"I'd say someone named Julia Lee owned it or was married to the owner at one time."

"Probably. I just know they make the best damn biscuit I have ever eaten."

"I think I might have to agree with that, Cliff."

After we finished, Cliff looked at me. "You need a bathroom break before we start?"

"No, I think I am good until Macon."

"Okay, then off we go."

A few minutes later, we were driving north on I-75. Cliff turned the radio down. "You know I like that song, but I think we need to talk."

"Okay."

"Michael, I do believe we are safely out of range of your mom's radar, so you need to tell me just what the hell we are doing."

"Cliff, we are going to North Carolina to clean up the area around the lake house so the family can go there in a month or so."

"Yes, but why exactly are we doing this, Michael?"

"It is complicated, Cliff, and I was trying to think of how to explain—"

"You mean when you were snoring?"

"Okay, maybe I did fall asleep. Remember, Cliff, I have two girls under six, so a good night's sleep is rare. But before the nap, I was trying to think of a way to explain it all to you."

"Well, Michael, I have always found the simplest way was to answer the question asked, which was why are we going to North Carolina? Take your time, do the best you can, and I think, between the two of us, we can sort it out."

"Okay, but this has to stay between us."

"Now you sound like your mom. Michael, you should know you can trust me, and I am not sure who I would be talking to in North Carolina. I don't know a lot of people there, and definitely none I would be discussing family business with."

"You're right. It's just that I worry someone will try to stop me, and I can't let that happen."

"Okay, so explain. I am listening, Michael."

"Three weeks ago, I found some letters in Mom's attic. Becky and I were looking for this ornament that Mom felt she had to have to use as a tree topper. Cliff, the letters were from Caitlin, the girl from Scotland."

"I remember her all right."

"Hard to forget."

"Yep, not your finest hour. Sleeping with someone in your parents' house and not going back to your bedroom before Becky arrives."

"For the sake of accuracy, it was my bedroom, so Caitlin should have been the one who went back to her bedroom."

"Okay, so you found some letters from her, then what?"

"There were five letters, and, Cliff, I had only received one. So I took the letter with no envelope, slipped it in my pocket, and took it home. When I read the letter, I realized the one I thought Caitlin had written me fifteen years earlier was most likely a fake."

"Why do you say that?"

"Several reasons, Cliff. First, the handwriting didn't match. When you put the two letters beside each other, it is obvious. Second, why was there no envelope on the letter I took from the attic?"

"Someone could have thrown it away."

"Or used it to put the fake letter in."

"Maybe!"

"Think about it, Cliff. It would make it look like the real thing."

"Yeah, maybe."

"And finally, the content of the letter from the attic was wrong. In the letter, Caitlin was upset about something I had written her. Cliff, I never wrote her a letter that would have upset her, so they must have written her a letter similar to the one I received."

"Sounds like you may be right. What about the other letters you left?"

"I went back to Twin Oaks when Mom was out of town with a friend and got them."

"And?"

"They confirmed what I thought. Caitlin still cared for me. The thing that was troubling was in the first letter I took, Caitlin said she was pregnant, just not exactly."

"Michael, either she was pregnant, or she wasn't."

"She didn't say she was pregnant. She said the baby moved."

"Okay, I think that qualifies as pregnant."

"Do you realize what that means? There is a good chance I have a child. A child that is fourteen years old that I knew nothing about. That's why I have to go to Scotland, to apologize to Caitlin and hopefully to see my child."

"Have you told anyone else?"

"I asked Tom for her address and the place she worked, but I never told him I was going to see her."

"I don't think you have to worry about Tom. He's someone you can trust."

"I do intend to tell Christy and Mom when I return, but I didn't think I could deal with that before I made the trip."

"Michael, I am not so sure you would be making the trip if you told them before you left."

"Why do you think I am telling them after I get back?"

"Well, the fact that you are going to tell them sounds good. Now how does that change the plans we talked about a few days ago?"

"We still go to Cherokee Landscaping and Grading when we get to Murphy to make sure they are going to start with the cleanup first thing Tuesday. Then we will go to the property to finalize the list of things we need them to do. Early Tuesday morning, I drive to Atlanta and fly to Scotland. Hopefully, I will be able to see Caitlin and my child and then fly back no later than Friday. I told Christy I would call or text her during the day when I had a chance. I will just call you each day to get an update on the progress being made."

"I am sure there will be things we will have to work out, but it sounds doable. The main problem I have with the new plan is, I was looking forward to some quality fishing time with you, Michael."

"I promise to make it up to you later, Cliff."

"I will hold you to it, but you might change your mind when you hear what I have to say. You see, son, you are not the only one who needs to straighten a few things out. I promised Walter not to say anything to you about it, but since you know most of the story, I don't think he would mind."

"What are you talking about?"

"You have a son, Michael."

"A son."

"Yes, your mom and dad went to Scotland after you started the year in that military school. Caitlin's father had called Walter and told him she was pregnant, so Walter and Peggy flew over to talk with Caitlin's parents. Later, when the child was born, they called and told your parents it was a boy."

"Cliff, I don't understand. Why…why didn't they tell me?"

"Michael, I don't know. I did tell Walter I didn't think it was right, keeping you in the dark, especially after you turned twenty-one. By that time, you had turned things around. You were doing great in college and about to begin your last year. That was more than a year before you started seeing Christy. But we all knew where Peggy stood on the subject, and Walter must have also thought it best to leave things as they were. Just never think your dad didn't have it in him to stand up to your mom. Like I said, he must have felt it was best to leave things as they were."

"It's just hard to believe they would…" I stopped as a thought occurred to me. "Did Dad ever say what was discussed when they met the Campbells?"

"No, but he did say he wasn't pleased with how things had gone."

"Did he say why?"

"No, but I don't believe it had anything to do with the Campbells. I never heard your dad say anything bad about them, and I do think he would have mentioned it if the Campbells had said or done something he thought was wrong."

"Maybe it was Mom. It was probably tough for Dad. You know how Mom can be. She is very controlling at times."

"Controlling, hell. A tyrant is what she is!"

I laughed. "At least you didn't have to live with her, Cliff."

"I am not so sure both of us would have survived. I just know that I would hate to be the one who stood between Peggy and something she wanted."

"I agree, and I have plenty of firsthand experience of her in action."

"Yes, but… I shouldn't say any more."

"Cliff, what is it?"

"I'll tell you but remember it stays in the cab of this truck."

"Understood."

"Let's go back a few years. Do you recall finding out about your dad's first wife?"

"Yes, that was a shock. Becky came storming into the house, holding a wedding picture and yelling at Mom, 'Is this Dad marrying another woman?'"

"I am sure it was a shock, but you need to remember the truth, quite often, was blurred or, in this case, omitted when Peggy was involved. So let's go back and give you a version you probably haven't heard."

"Okay."

"Michael, your dad, Walter, was a bright man. He graduated with honors from the university with a degree in forestry and came to Roseville in the late '50s. He started working as a forestry agent and loved his work, but he had a dream. Walter saved every penny he could while waiting for the right opportunity to come along. It came in the spring of 1962. Samuel Riddle decided it was time for him to get out of the lumber business. He had made a great deal of money in lumber, but his sons showed no interest in the business. I believe one became a lawyer, and the other, a dentist. Samuel wanted to sell the business, enjoy life with his wife, and spend more time with the grandkids. Walter knew the business had real potential, and old Samuel liked Walter. But he said he wouldn't sell for less than $400,000. With some negotiations, Walter got Samuel to agree to a deal. He would get a lawyer to draw up an agreement where Walter would pay Samuel $100,000 initially and pay him $50,000 annually for the next seven years. Samuel was pleased with the deal since he would be getting $50,000 over asking and his accountant said this was also great for tax purposes. The only problem was, Walter had only saved a little over $10,000 and no bank would loan him the money he needed."

My phone rang, and I saw it was Christy as I accepted the call.

"Hi, everything okay?"

"Yes, it's the girls, Michael. They wanted to see where you were before going to day care."

"I think we are a few miles from Cordele. Hey, girls. Love you."

"Love you, Daddy!" Brittney and Nicole yelled in unison.

"Well, you two be good today. Now let me talk to your mom."

"Love you, Michael. Look, I need to run, or they will be late!"

"Love you too, Christy." I could hear a catch in her voice and hoped it was due to poor reception. *When will Christy realize I have forgiven her and move on from the problem in our past?*

Cliff waited until Michael put his phone on the console and then started again. "Walter had been engaged to Patsy Coleman for about three months, and one night, Walter discussed the deal with her father, Roger Coleman. At the time, Roger was a successful builder in the area. He was also a shrewd businessman, and he knew the deal Samuel had offered Walter was a good one. So Roger agreed to back Walter for a stake in the company. Roger wanted a 50 percent stake. But Walter was able to talk him into accepting a 40 percent stake, and the deal was made. I know all this because I was working at the bank Walter used. Walter would never have been able to get a loan for that amount without Roger's backing. Three months later, your dad married Patsy, and the Williams Lumber Company opened shortly afterward. The lumber business was a natural fit for Walter. I have known few men who loved their work as he did, and he built a team spirit within his employees that was special. He held the usual cookouts and Christmas celebrations, but he did more than that. Walter wasn't just their boss; he was thought of as one of them. He worked alongside them. Some days, he would go out where a crew was cutting the trees and work all day with them. Then the next day, he might work with the men at the yard where they took the trees, stripped them, and cut them into boards. If something went wrong with any of the equipment, he was there, and soon he had learned how to maintain the equipment as well as those who worked with it every day. Your dad was also a true salesman. He had the rare ability to put into words why someone should sell their timber to Williams Lumber and why they should buy the finished product from him. He was so engaging and such a dynamo those first ten years or so. Anyone who worked with Walter knew he was special, and most would say they just plain enjoyed being around him. Michael, he built a loyalty in his workforce I have not seen before or since."

"Cliff, how do you think he did that?"

"Michael, your dad cared about his people, and they knew it was genuine. The sad part was, while his business thrived, his relationship with Patsy suffered. Walter was working twelve-hour days and using his home as a place to eat and sleep. It wasn't good for their marriage, and I think Patsy made a mistake."

"What do you mean?"

"Patsy and I were talking one night at a cook-out held at Roger's house, and she made a comment about how she would be glad when Walter worked less hours. I told her not to worry about that. As soon as they had a few kids, Walter would change. When I said that, she let me know there would be no kids until he started working normal hours. Then she said, 'I've made sure of that.' I didn't say any more since I could tell it was a sensitive topic. But I thought it was a mistake. A mistake that cost her Walter. Walter loved you kids, and it definitely changed his priorities when you and Becky were born. I believe it would have been the same if Patsy had chosen to start a family."

"Strange how things work out. Where was Mom at this time?"

"Your mom started working in the office two years after Williams Lumber Company opened up. She was only nineteen, but she was sharp and quickly mastered any task she was assigned. She started in bookkeeping, but her real talent emerged when she moved into sales. Now you must remember your dad was dividing his time between the office, the lumberyard, and the field. He often relied on certain people in those three different areas to keep him updated. In her second year at Williams, Peggy was his go-to person in the office. Now I am not saying anything went on between them, but anyone who saw them working together would have thought it was a little more than a boss/employee relationship. There was a chemistry that developed between them to the point where Peggy was actually making big money transactions before receiving his approval. Listen, your mom had a phenomenal memory and great instincts. She knew all the reps—"

I interrupted, "Did Dad ever call her on any of these decisions she made without his consent?"

"If he did, it was rare. Your father viewed Peggy as a trusted member of the Williams team, and he thought if she made the decision thinking it was best for the company, then he would have done the same."

"So what about the divorce?"

"Michael, I think Patsy got tired of waiting for Walter to put his family on an equal footing with the business, so she filed for divorce."

"She did?"

"Yep. Irreconcilable differences was what Walter told me she had the lawyer put on the divorce papers. That was a sad day. He calls me at the bank and asks if I can go to lunch at eleven thirty. After I said I could, he tells me to meet him in the City Park so we can talk in private. He said he would pick up two barbecue plates and meet me there. This was unusual since your dad typically ate with the crew in the field or at the office, so I knew something was wrong. When I got to the park, I found him sitting at one of the benches with the food, and he says, 'We should eat first and then talk.' I knew it was bad because I could tell he had been crying. When we were finished, Walter handed me a note. He told me he found it on the kitchen table when he went home the previous night. I opened it and saw Patsy's name at the bottom. It was only three lines. Basically, she said she couldn't continue in the marriage and wanted nothing but her freedom.

Walter had tried to contact Patsy at Roger's to talk with her, but Roger told him there wasn't any need for talk. The papers were being drawn up, and the quicker this was over, the better it would be for all. As I stared at the note and listened to Walter, I realized the marriage was over. I told him if she wouldn't talk, then there wasn't much hope. The note left little doubt. Two months later, the divorce was final. The next week, Roger told Walter he no longer wanted to be a part of Williams Lumber and asked him for $1 million for his stake in the company. Walter said he would agree as long as half went to Patsy. A little over a year later, Walter married your mom."

"Do you think Mom was a cause of the divorce?"

"If you are asking me if anything went on between Walter and Peggy prior to the divorce, I would say no. Your dad wasn't wired like that, Michael. However, I went to Williams Lumber several times in the years Peggy was working before the divorce, and what I saw was a closeness between the two that was not good for Walter's marriage. I am sure you're aware your mom has a way of nudging people into complying with her wishes, often without the person realizing what she has done. The victim often thinks it was their decision."

"Yes, I have seen her in action too often."

"Yep, yep. I have seen my share as well. I joined Williams Lumber three years before you were born. The company had grown so much your father wanted a comptroller he could trust. Eight years at the bank watching promotions go to others with influential family or friends made it an easy choice. If I were being honest, it also did not hurt that Walter offered me more money."

"But, Cliff, why did it take so long to find out Dad had been married to someone before Mom?"

"Yeah, I sort of left that out, didn't I? Probably because I am so conditioned to omit that part of the story. Well, the first year of the marriage, Peggy gets pregnant, and by this time, the Williams brand was known all over the southeast. Peggy would not tolerate anything that would tarnish the public image of the company. So she made sure everyone knew that any mention of Patsy was taboo. As they say, Michael, history is written by the victor, and Peggy made damn sure that history did not include Patsy."

"What happened to Patsy?"

"She remarried a few years after the divorce. Her husband is some big farmer who lives about thirty miles from Roseville. The last I heard was they had several kids and were doing great. Michael, Patsy was a good girl. Don't believe anyone that tells you she wasn't."

"Unfortunately, she got in Mom's way. That does not usually work out well."

"No, it does not, but like I said, I never saw your mom do anything."

"But, Cliff, that is what you would expect. I never thought the letter was a fake until I found the other. I still do not know for certain it was Mom, but my money is on her."

"I think you may be right."

I glanced at a sign that read Forsyth—5 Miles. "Looks like our exit is coming up."

"Yep, you want to find a place to take a break?"

"Sure, and, Cliff, thanks for giving me a chance to see Caitlin and my son."

"Did I say I would?" Cliff said as he grinned.

"I guess I just thought you would."

"Just kidding, Michael. I think it is the right thing to do. So yes, I will be your partner in crime. But you have to keep our little conversation between us."

"I will try, Cliff."

"That is all I can ask."

Chapter Seven

I t was one fifteen when Cliff and I walked into Cherokee Landscaping and Grading. I had spoken to the owner, Junior Phelps, last week, and if people look like they sound on the phone, then he was the one sitting behind the desk, talking on the phone when we entered.

"Hey, I gotta go," the man sitting at the desk said. After he laid the phone on the desk, he smiled and asked, "What can I do for you'ns?"

"I'm Michael Williams, and this is Cliff Williams. I called last week and spoke to a Mr. Phelps. We—"

"Junior, please."

"As I was saying, I called about contracting your services to clean up our property."

"Yep. Your place is out past the Hanging Dog Community. Earl's been out there to check it out."

"Yes. We just wanted to know if you were going to be able to start tomorrow."

"Yep. Sent Earl up there today to dig a far pit. His pa owned a piece of that land years back."

"Okay." I looked at Cliff and grinned. I could tell I was flying solo on this mission, so I continued, "So you'll be there tomorrow."

"Yes, sir. We'ns did the work for your pa back in the late seventies when he bought it."

"Yes, Mom did say Dad was pleased with your work."

"That's when my pa ran the business. I was just a lap baby back then."

"Do you get good TV reception up here?"

"No cable where you'ns is, but you can run an antenner up to the top of the ridge."

"I guess that answers that. Thanks. We'll see you tomorrow then."

"Yep. We'll be there when the sun comes up."

I started to turn to leave and then thought of something. "Do you know a place nearby where I could rent a truck?"

Junior beamed and said, "Junior's Auto."

"Where is that?"

"Right here. Trucks are out back. Just go pick out one, and I'll bring you the keys."

"Thanks."

As Cliff and I walked around the trailer, Cliff started laughing. "What the hell. I thought we had an accent, Michael."

"Don't think it is called an accent, Cliff."

"And then you asked him about the TV reception. We are lucky he didn't get that, or we might be looking for another crew."

"I think Junior likes the money, Cliff."

"You're probably right. Just a word to the wise. Never, and I do mean never, make fun of them. I remember your dad telling me about the locals who have lived in the area for generations after he had been up here several times. He said it took a long time for them to accept a newcomer into their community, if they ever did. Michael, they consider us outsiders, and they refer to people from our part of the country as flatlanders. So I think it would be smart to keep that in mind. I guess what I'm trying to say is, we need to keep Junior happy."

"I guess I just wasn't—"

Cliff interrupted, "Yep, I think I like the Dodge."

I turned and saw Junior walking out the back of the trailer.

"Good deal," Junior said as he threw a set of keys to Cliff.

"What about the paperwork?" I asked.

"You'ns are good."

I followed Cliff as he drove out of the city of Murphy. In a few miles, I saw a sign that read Hanging Dog Community, and I knew we were close. After several more minutes, we turned onto a narrow dirt road that wound its way back to a small mountain in the distance. I knew where we were now, and as the truck started up an incline, I looked across the lake below and could see a house in the distance—the house my father built when I was a child.

At one time, it had been a pilgrimage the family would make several times each year. Dad had fallen in love with the mountains of North Carolina when he was a student in college, and he took great pleasure in sharing this love with his family. I had many special memories of these times before Becky's marriage. I remembered the fishing and the hikes we would take to see some obscure treasure of nature Dad had found, but most of all, I recalled the colors—these brilliant colors—that covered the hills and valleys. I would never forget how Becky described it to a seven-year-old one autumn as the two of us stood on a small hill and looked across the landscape—God's palette.

Chapter Eight

It had been two hours since I parked my truck in long-term parking. The careful scrutiny of both passengers and their baggage added an extra hour to the wait time, and as usual, I was anxious as I settled into my seat, waiting for the plane to taxi over to the runway. I texted Christy earlier while I was at a bar in the terminal. A preflight drink seemed to steady my nerves. It was not that I had a fear of flying. But a transatlantic flight offered ample opportunities for turbulence, so I figured, why take the risk?

As I sat in my seat, I thought back to the conversation with Christy when I first brought up the idea of my going to North Carolina. She had initially been against the plan, but I anticipated that reaction and was prepared. I reassured her all was fine and countered her objections with the argument that this would make it possible for us to have some good quality time together as a family. The final selling point was that my cousin Cliff would be going with me to help with the project. Christy respected and trusted Cliff, and so she reluctantly agreed, but only after I promised to keep her and the girls posted on the daily progress. I knew it was just her way of checking on me, and I understood. It wouldn't present a problem since I would merely talk with Cliff before I called or texted Christy. I knew she was concerned and why. I often wondered how long it would be until we moved past our problem of three years ago.

I always dreamed of being the CEO of Williams Lumber Company, but I envisioned it would be in the distant future. I had worked at the company since I was a teenager in the summers. Then when

I graduated from college, I joined the company my father founded and I had grown to love. It was a great experience working with a successful company that took pride in producing a quality product and also providing hundreds of employees with a great life. I was soon accepted as a member of the Williams family, as Dad referred to his employees, and then I wasn't.

I had earned the respect of the members of this extended family, and I was enjoying being a part of this group when my father died. The shock of his death was devastating, not just to his immediate family. I had heard of charismatic military leaders inspiring such loyalty within the men under their command to a point that it bordered on adoration. I witnessed this firsthand at the visitation and funeral of Walter Williams. The men and women of Williams Lumber, from the secretary to the hardened workers in the field, all brought their families to pay homage to a man they revered. So when Mom asked me to assume the role as CEO, there was only one choice—I accepted.

I realized it was a mistake after a few weeks. I was not ready for such responsibility, and I missed the camaraderie with the employees that was absent in my new role. I finally approached Mom and convinced her she was more suited for the role. Unfortunately, I hadn't acted quickly enough. Christy and one of our best friends had an affair.

As I moved back into my role as a general supervisor, things soon returned to normal. There were no more late hours or last-minute trips to court a potential client that had emerged. There was a joy back in our home that had been missing, but I sensed something was not quite right with Christy. She should have been ecstatic since our second child was due in a few months.

When Nicole was born, Christy seemed to be more like the Christy before my stint as CEO, and for a few months, all was fine. Then one Saturday morning, we were outside enjoying the sunshine when Brittney, our eldest daughter, ran over to where Christy and I were playing with Nicole on a blanket. Brittney stared at Nicole for a moment and asked, "Why are Nicole's eyes different, Mommy?"

Christy picked Nicole up and said, "Well, Brittney, all babies can't have blue eyes." Brittney seemed satisfied with the answer, picked up her butterfly net, and started chasing a small butterfly that had violated her domain.

I could see the tears in the corners of Christy's eyes as she held Nicole in her arms. The remark by Brittney had hurt, but Christy had remained composed. I wondered if she would fare as well when others noticed the same thing Brittney had. Nicole was not my child.

Later, when the two girls were napping, we went out to sit on the back porch. Christy had struggled to speak, as she was choked with emotion. "I prayed, Michael. I prayed, and yet…"

A close friend of ours, Phil Parrish, had lost his wife to cancer shortly after my father died, and Christy would occasionally take him a meal. Several other friends were doing this as well. However, Christy was also suffering due to my absence at home. As a result, each served as a sympathetic ear for the other, and a short-lived affair had been the result. They both soon realized how wrong it was, but unfortunately, it was too late.

Initially, I was very angry with Christy, but I soon realized the affair was as much my fault as hers. I told her I understood and that I was still in love with her. I also assured her I would always consider Nicole my daughter. Though our relationship improved over the next few weeks, the guilt Christy still harbored undermined the trust we once shared. I asked her if she would consider going to a marriage counselor, but that conversation did not go well. What troubled me more was what Nicole might face in the future. Life can be cruel.

Chapter Nine

I arrived in Edinburgh at nine thirty. There had been a six-hour layover at Heathrow before I caught the connecting flight. I debated whether to get a room or not and decided it wasn't worth it. I would not make that mistake in the future. The security a room provides is worth the price.

After arriving in Edinburgh, I decided I would check into the hotel, get a shower, and eat before going to see Caitlin. I was exhausted and sleep-deprived after the experience at Heathrow, and I knew it would be wise to be at my best for the meeting with her. A warm shower and a good meal usually worked, and I hoped that would be the case this time. I also must confess there was another reason: I wanted to look my best when I saw Caitlin.

At one fifteen, I walked into the branch of the Royal Bank of Scotland where Tom said Caitlin was currently employed. As I looked around, I was thankful that it wasn't terribly busy. I then walked up to a teller's window.

"Can I help you, sir?"

"Yes, I would like to speak to Caitlin, Caitlin Campbell. You know, she may be married, so her last name may have changed." I knew I sounded like an idiot and mentally kicked myself for not asking Tom if she was married.

"Sir, we do have a Ms. Campbell. She is the assistant to the manager of this branch, but unfortunately, she is not here today. I do apologize."

"Could I speak to someone—"

"I believe the person you need to speak with is Ms. Frasier. If you will take a seat, I'll check with her. May I have your name, sir?"

"Michael Williams."

"Okay, Mr. Williams, it may take a few minutes."

"Thank you," I said and then took a seat. I felt relieved that Caitlin seemed to be doing well. The bank also appeared to be a pleasant workplace, and that served to ease my conscience. A few minutes later, I saw a young woman walking in my direction. She smiled when she noticed I was looking at her, and I stood as she came near.

"Hi, my name is Erin Frasier, and I understand you wished to see Ms. Campbell."

"Yes."

"I do apologize, Mr. Williams, but she will not be in today. If this concerns a financial matter, I am sure I or another member of our staff can assist you."

"No, no, this is not business-related. I just needed to see her—actually, to apologize to her for something."

"I see."

"Could you possibly give me her cell number?"

"I'm sorry, Mr. Williams, but that is against bank policy. I'm sure you understand."

"Yes."

"She is scheduled to work tomorrow, if that helps."

"It does and thank you, Ms. Frasier."

"You're welcome, and I do hope you have a pleasant day."

"Thanks."

And that was just the beginning of my failed attempts to see Caitlin. I then called a taxi to take me to her parents' address. I thought it was unlikely she still lived with her parents, but Tom said that was the last address he had for Caitlin.

As I rode in the taxi, I began to think about what I was going to say to Caitlin's parents to convince them to help me, and I soon realized how foolish that notion was. Why would her parents help me? Considering the way my mom most likely treated them, I should consider myself lucky if they merely slammed the door in my face. Facing them was not going to be an easy task, but it was my best chance to see Caitlin. So I had no choice. Whatever humiliation I had to suffer would be worth it. Caitlin deserved to know the truth.

When I arrived at the address Tom had given me, I asked the driver to wait while I checked to see if anyone was home. When no one answered the doorbell or my knocking on the door, I went to the neighbor's house. After knocking on the door, I heard noises from inside and hoped I hadn't disturbed their nap. A few moments passed, and then I heard the lock being turned. As the door opened slowly, it revealed an older man peering at me as if he were trying to decide if he should close the door in my face.

"I'm not buying anything," the old man finally said.

"Sir, I'm just looking for the Campbells."

"They live next door. Good day," the man said as he started closing the door.

"Sir, they aren't home. I just thought you might know where they are."

The door stopped, leaving a narrow slit. "Colin did say something a few days ago about the family going to the beach when he was off. Is today Wednesday?"

"Yes, sir."

"Then I think they might be at the beach. Colin is off most Wednesdays."

"Do you happen to know which beach?"

"Sorry. He didn't say. There are quite a few of them."

"Thank you, sir, and I'm sorry if I disturbed you."

"That's okay."

The door closed, and I walked back to the taxi. It would be impossible to find them and could be hours before they returned. Caitlin was scheduled to work tomorrow, and that was when I would hopefully see her. Settling into the back seat, I glanced at my watch and realized I needed to call Cliff and get an update before I talked with Christy and the kids. "Take me back to Old Town, please."

Chapter Ten

Caitlin heard her phone's ringtone and picked it up off the towel. She saw it was Erin. "I need to answer this, Mum. It may be work."

"Sure."

"Yes, Erin, can you hear me?" Caitlin said as she walked a short distance away from where her mum was sitting in a chair.

"Yes, we just had a visitor I thought you might be interested in hearing about."

"An auditor?"

"No, visitor. Someone who wanted to see you."

"Who?"

"A Mr. Michael Williams."

"Who did you say?"

"Michael Williams. He said he wanted to see you and apologize. Judging by his accent, Cat, I think it may be your friend from the States. That was his name, wasn't it?"

"Bloody hell. I do not want his apology. I just want him to stay out of my life."

"Cat, you didn't say he was so good-looking."

"Good looks do not make up for what he did."

"Anyway, I think he plans to come back tomorrow, and he asked for your number."

"Erin, please tell me you did not give that man my mobile number."

"No! No, I didn't."

"At least you did one thing right, and if I come in tomorrow, I will be unavailable for any meeting with him. Understood?"

"Yes, boss. Enjoy the rest of your day."

"Bye."

Caitlin walked back over to her mother and took a seat in the chair beside her.

"Everything okay at work, dear?"

"Yes, work's fine. It's just Michael."

"Michael?"

"Yes, Michael Williams. The one from Roseville, Georgia."

"Is he here?"

"Yes, he is, and he wants to talk with me. That's the last thing I need at this time. I don't think I can take any more."

"Caitlin, he may want to see Ryan. That is natural for a father."

"It's a little late, Mum. Ryan can't find out about him. I often wish we had never said anything to the Williams family about my being pregnant. I think it would have been better. Michael could say something and ruin the life we have worked so hard to give Ryan. We can't allow that to happen."

"Of course, dear. It's just that it might be hard to deny Michael a chance to at least see his son. You know his father fell in love with Ryan when he saw him, and he insisted on sending us money each month to help with expenses."

"He came once, Mum."

"I think that had more to do with Peggy and the health issues he had. He loved Ryan."

"Fine, but Michael made it clear that he thought it best if we went our separate ways."

"Maybe he has had a change of heart. You were both so young, and he may now realize what a mistake he made by not allowing Ryan to be a part of his life."

"That would be a drastic change. Do you remember the letter he sent me?"

"Yes, Caitlin. It was horrible, but like I said, you both were so young. Maybe he regrets what he did."

"Well, all I have to say is it's a little late, and I don't think he has the right to have any say in the matter. I just wish he would have stayed out of our lives."

"Just meet with Michael and tell him how you feel, dear. I think that is better than avoiding him. You have nothing to be ashamed of. Ryan is a young man that would make any parent proud. Your dad and I can pick Ryan up and take him for an ice cream. You know how he likes surprises."

"That sounds good."

"The last thing you need is to let this upset you."

"I know, Mum."

"I just worry. You know I love you, Caitlin."

"Love you too, Mum."

Caitlin looked down at the beach where Ryan and her father were fishing. She picked up her camera and took a picture of the two of them. It was hard for her to believe how much Ryan had grown. Just three years earlier, he was six inches shorter than Colin, and after a similar day, Colin had carried an exhausted Ryan to the car after he had fallen asleep in one of the chairs. Ryan was now three inches taller than his grandfather and showed no signs of slowing down.

Caitlin's thoughts were interrupted by shouts from Colin and Ryan. She looked in their direction and saw a large fish jump out of the water. Kathleen and Caitlin hurried down to the water's edge and arrived as Ryan was pulling the fish out of the water.

"Look, Mum. Look what I caught," Ryan said as he smiled and looked at Kathleen.

"She is a big one," Kathleen said.

"I think we need a picture! Mum and Dad, stand beside Ryan." As she looked through the camera's lens and saw the smile on Ryan's face, Caitlin knew this was the kind of moment she would always cherish. It just hurt when she was reminded of what she was being denied. But at least she was with him, and that was what mattered.

Chapter Eleven

C aitlin stared into the mirror. *Why am I so nervous, and what do I have to be nervous about?* She had decided to see Michael. He deserved to be told exactly how she felt about him. He told her she was the one he loved, yet that all changed when she returned to Scotland. Michael had a sudden change of heart and felt it best if they both went back to their life before they had met. That made no sense. He had lied to her. He lied to get what all men wanted, and that disgusted her. How could she have thought he was different? It still hurt after all these years. She couldn't forgive him for the lies or forgive herself for being so foolish.

Caitlin glanced into the mirror one last time to be sure she still had it. She wanted Michael to regret his decision not to be a part of her and Ryan's life, but most of all, she wanted him to regret his rejection of her. That was why she wanted to be sure she still had it. Caitlin smiled as she heard a light tap on the door to her room.

"Yes."

"Mum said we need to come down. Breakfast is ready, and you know how she is."

"Yes, I most certainly do," Caitlin said as she walked over and opened the door.

"My, you look good."

"Does that mean I don't always look good? Remember, this is important for future reference. I'm sure you are getting the looks from a lot of the girls."

"No—what?" Ryan managed as his cheeks turned red.

"Just kidding, and you do look handsome yourself. Let's go make Mum happy."

Ryan smiled and turned to walk to the stairs down the hall from the room his sister had been using the past three weeks.

Caitlin started for the door and suddenly felt dizzy. She tried to say something to Ryan. But it was too late, everything went black, and she fell to the floor.

Chapter Twelve

The previous day was almost a complete waste. The only things that salvaged it were my calls to Cliff and Christy. At least everything seemed to be going well in North Carolina and at home. I considered calling it quits and catching a flight back, but I decided, since I was in Scotland, I would make one more attempt. I had taken the precaution of writing Caitlin a letter of apology, which I was going to leave at the bank if she was not there. Then I would try her parents' home once more, and if the results were the same, I was done. I could be home tomorrow, and at least I could say I made the effort.

I walked into the bank at ten thirty. It was not any busier than it had been the previous day, and I was able to walk up to one of the tellers' windows.

"May I help you, sir?" the young man asked.

"Would it be possible to speak to Ms. Caitlin Campbell?"

"I don't believe she has come in yet, sir, but let me check."

The young man walked over to a telephone and made a call. After he briefly spoke with someone, he returned to the window. "Ms. Frasier asked if you would come to her office. It is down the corridor to your left, sir."

As I walked over to the corridor, I prepared myself for the anticipated disappointment. Erin was standing in the doorway of what I assumed was her office.

"Please come in, Mr. Williams."

"Thank you. Your coworker said Caitlin wasn't here yet."

"Yes, and I am at a loss to explain why. She assured me when I talked with her yesterday that it was her intention to work today."

"So you talked with her after our conversation?"

"Yes, and she made it very clear to me that she had no desire to see you or talk with you."

"I can understand. Would you please be kind enough to give her this for me?" I said as I took the letter from my pocket and handed it to Erin. "If she changes her mind, I am staying at the Sheraton."

"Yes," Erin said as she took the letter.

"Also, could you tell her I am sorry if my coming has upset her?"

"I will. Have a safe trip home, Mr. Williams."

"Thank you," I said, and for a moment, I just stood there. I could tell Erin wasn't sincere. I had no idea how much she knew, but if she was a close friend of Caitlin, she probably knew enough.

I walked out of the bank, called a taxi, and went to her parents' house. I was going to make a final effort. If no one was home, I would find a place to eat, get a drink, and take a walk to kill some time until I had to leave for the airport. I checked earlier, and there was a flight to London departing at six thirty, with a connecting flight to Atlanta.

As the taxi turned onto the street and pulled up to the house, I saw a young man walk up and go inside. *Finally,* I thought.

I hurried up to the door and knocked. In a short time, the door opened, and the young man I had seen walk into the house smiled at me and asked, "Can I help you, sir?"

"Yes, I am looking for Caitlin Campbell."

"I'm sorry. She is not here. She—"

"Is her child here?"

The boy had a puzzled expression on his face. "I think you must have the wrong Caitlin Campbell. My sister has no kids, and she isn't married. It is an honest mistake. I know of two other women with the same name, and I'm certain there are more."

I was frustrated and confused and wasn't sure what to say. "Yes, I guess I made a mistake. I'm sorry I bothered you."

"It's okay, and I do hope you find her."

"Thanks."

And that was it. I was suddenly very angry. I had been thwarted at each attempt. Not only was I unable to see Caitlin, but she also knew I was in Scotland and had asked me to leave her alone. I did not understand. The boy had said his sister was named Caitlin, and the neighbor had confirmed Colin's family still lived at this address. What if the boy was unaware that Caitlin had a child? As I opened the cab door, a thought occurred to me. *I could describe her to the boy and then...* But I stopped because I realized I would be describing a sixteen-year-old Caitlin to him. As I turned to look back at the house, I saw the young man walk out to the road, get in a car, and leave. I took a seat in the taxi. "Take me to the Sheraton in Old Town."

"Yes, sir."

I was angry and was trying to avoid thinking about my next step, which was obvious. However, I had only one thought: *What the hell have you done with our child, Caitlin?*

Chapter Thirteen

Erin called Caitlin for the second time in the past hour, and once again, it went to voice mail. She knew that was unusual since Caitlin was very attached to her phone. She could not understand why Caitlin had not answered. With her recent absences due to the medical issue, Caitlin often received bank-related calls throughout the day, so keeping her phone nearby had been a priority the past few weeks.

Erin looked at the letter on her desk and, for a moment, considered ripping it to pieces. She was startled from her thoughts as her phone buzzed, indicating a text. She picked up her phone, opened it, and read.

Caitlin will not be in today. She had a second episode and we are concerned. She is in hospital and says she will call you later today. In all the confusion we left her phone at home.

Erin stared at the text from Kathleen and considered calling but then realized it might not be wise. Instead, she texted back: *How is Cat?*

She seems ok. The doctor said he wanted her to stay overnight.

Erin replied, *Tell her I will see her after work,* and quickly received another text.

Ok. Bye.

Erin thought it best not to say anything about Michael's second visit or the letter at this time. What if his arrival caused this second episode? She looked at the letter again then picked it up. *I'll decide before I go see Cat,* she thought as she slipped the letter into her bag.

Chapter Fourteen

I decided I would take a walk to pass the time and hopefully relieve some of the stress from being frustrated in my attempts to see Caitlin. I knew in a few hours I would be going to the airport and leave Caitlin and Scotland behind. The letter would at least let Caitlin know I still cared for her as well as let her know it was my family, not me, who had rejected her. The pain I felt when I first read the actual letter she had written was still there.

It started raining, and I darted up the steps of a small chapel I was beside. As I stood under the shelter, the door to the chapel opened and a priest or father stepped out. He smiled when he noticed me. "I got caught in the rain. I hope you don't mind if I use your shelter."

"No, that's fine. It should pass in a few minutes."

"I guess you are familiar with the weather here?"

"To be honest, I was listening to the weather on the radio a few minutes ago. It said there would be a brief shower."

"Is it Father?"

"Yes, I'm serving the church in Father McDonald's absence. He recently had surgery and will be out for a few weeks while he is recovering. Can I help you with anything?"

"Father, I'm not Catholic or much of anything, to be honest. My wife takes our girls to a church most Sundays, and I attend often enough to put an end to any rumors that may be circulating."

"That's interesting. I think I see you as a potential member. Please, let's take a seat inside."

I followed him as he walked back into the small sanctuary, and we took a seat on a pew in the rear of the church.

"My name is Father James."

"I am Michael Williams and thank you for your hospitality. I definitely need some."

"It is the least I can do. Do you live nearby?"

"No, sir, I am just visiting. I am from Roseville, Georgia."

"Oh, so you are from the States?"

"Yes, sir."

"Well, for future reference, a wise man once told me the way to prepare for the conditions in Scotland was to dress for the four seasons each day, and I soon found he was right."

"I'll try to remember that if I come back."

"Pardon me for making an observation, but you seem troubled. Are you having difficulties?"

"That would be an understatement."

"Would you like to talk about it, son?"

"I wouldn't know where to start, Father."

"Just tell me what is troubling you."

I didn't know this man, and I doubted I would ever see him again after I walked out the door. So I told him. "I came to Scotland to see a girl I had a relationship with over fifteen years ago. I felt compelled to come after finding a letter that completely changed what I thought was the truth concerning that time. I am now certain our relationship was ended as a result of the actions taken by my parents. You see, Father, the girl and I were both led to believe that the other thought it was impossible to continue."

"So the parents deceived both of you?"

"My parents."

"And you came here for what purpose?"

"To see her and to apologize."

"That is commendable. I'm sure it was quite disturbing when you learned of this deception. Does the girl know?"

"No, I'm sure she was a victim of the deception just as I was."

"That is sad."

"Yes, it has been very frustrating. I have tried to see her several times, but I have been unsuccessful."

"Could it possibly be that she doesn't wish to see you?"

"I'm sure of that."

"Oh."

"Yes, I was told by a coworker who, I suspect, is also a friend that she knew I was in Edinburgh and did not care to meet with me."

"Well, maybe it is for the best."

"Father, I don't think you understand. It is very confusing. She has no idea she was duped."

"Son, are you trying to…to…"

"Father, all I am trying to do is correct a misconception she has and apologize to her. That is all."

"That is comforting. I worry about the family of today. There are so many issues in this new era that impact its stability."

"Father, I am a happily married man with two young girls I adore. I just felt that she should know the truth."

"Does your wife know that you are in Scotland?"

I looked down at my hands. "No, sir, she doesn't."

"Do you intend to tell her?"

"I was, but if I never see the girl, I may not. What would you suggest?"

"In a situation like this, it is a difficult choice, but I think honesty always wins out. I feel your intentions were noble, but unfortunately, perception often depends on the individual. I hope your wife is very understanding."

"We have a good relationship that has weathered some rough patches."

"Then my prayer will be that your marriage is not harmed by your actions."

"Thank you, Father."

"I believe the rain has stopped, but there is no hurry. I have enjoyed our talk."

"I would have to say I did as well. But I have a flight to catch, so I need to get back to the hotel."

"Have a safe trip, son."

"Thank you, Father, and I hope you enjoy your time here."

As I started out, I noticed a small box for donations and took some money out of my pocket and put it in the box. *A consulting fee*, I thought as I made my way down the wet steps and started toward the hotel.

Chapter Fifteen

aitlin heard a slight tapping on the door. "You can come in."

Erin pushed the door open and entered the dimly lit room. "I thought I would come by and bring you something to cheer you up."

"Cake?"

"No, but close. Chocolates!" Erin said as she revealed the box she had been hiding behind her back.

"Now all we need is a couple of glasses of wine and a sad movie."

"Girls' night out at hospital. Maybe next time."

"I'll hold you to it."

"That's a deal. So when do you get released, Cat?"

"The doctor thought it best to stay overnight to be safe, and if I have a good night, then I can go home tomorrow."

"Any idea about what's next?"

"I see a specialist next week."

"Nothing beats the efficiency of the NHS."

"You sound like my doctor."

"It would be funny if it wasn't well deserved."

"I just want to get back to a normal life."

"Well, if it helps, raising a little girl on my own has made me redefine normal."

"Jenny is worth it."

"Yes, she is. Where is the family?"

"I told them to go home and get some rest. Mum and Dad were here most of the day, and Ryan came by to see me after school."

"Ryan is so cute and such a gentleman, Cat. My brother is a miserable lout. Of course, he is five years older. Pray your brother doesn't change."

"I think he will be fine."

"Has he thought about what he would like to do?"

"There is that club that is really trying to get him to commit to them, but he has wanted to be an engineer for so long. I think he wants to go to university to study that."

"Brains, good looks, and such a good athlete. Cat, what happened? They saved it all for him?"

"I have noticed I still get the looks, so you just mind your tongue, Erin Frasier!"

"Just kidding. I hate it, love, but I need to go. I have to pick up Jenny from my parents and get her home to start all over again."

"I understand."

Erin hugged Caitlin and set the box of chocolates on the table beside the bed. She then took the letter out of her bag and placed it with the chocolates. "The letter."

"Letter?"

"Michael came by again today and left it. I thought about tearing it up but decided I would allow you that pleasure. I need to go, Cat, but I'll see you tomorrow."

"Okay, love. Give Jenny a hug for me."

"I will, Cat, and you mind the doctors and nurses."

"No promises," Caitlin said as Erin hugged her again. After Erin walked out of the room, Caitlin picked up the box of chocolates and the letter. She set the chocolates back down and stared at the letter.

Chapter Sixteen

Caitlin was crying as the nurse entered the room.

"I need to check your…" The nurse stopped as she realized something was terribly wrong and hurried to Caitlin's bedside. "Is there a problem? Why didn't you call for me?"

"No, no, I'm fine," Caitlin managed as she tried to reassure the nurse while she continued to cry.

"Ms. Campbell, Dr. Morrison is one of the finest doctors on staff. Please don't worry. You have merely suffered a temporary setback."

"You don't understand. I am crying because I am happy."

"What?"

"For a long time, I have thought a person I loved had betrayed me, and I have just discovered I was wrong."

"Okay. You gave me quite a scare."

"I'm sorry."

"Nothing to be sorry about. Now let's see how you are doing."

As the nurse proceeded to check Caitlin's vitals, all Caitlin could think was, *How long is this going to take? I need to call Erin.*

When she finished, the nurse looked at Caitlin and said, "We have people on staff if you need to talk with someone."

"No, I'm fine." Caitlin worried that Michael had already left Scotland. She picked up her phone as the nurse started for the door.

"Remember, please call me if you need anything."

"Yes, I will."

Erin answered on the second ring. "Hi, love, still thinking about that cake?"

"Erin, you have to stop him!"

"Who, Cat?"

"Michael. Please, stop him. I need to see him."

"Are you sure?"

"Yes."

"I'll try, Cat, but you do realize he may already be gone?"

"Yes, just please try."

"Okay, I'll call you back when I know something."

Fifteen minutes later, Erin called. Caitlin accepted the call but hesitated to speak, fearful of the news Erin had.

"Cat? You there?" Erin asked after a few moments of silence.

"Yes."

"You didn't say anything, so I wasn't sure the call went through."

"Is he gone?"

"His flight was boarding in ten minutes, so I had a friend who works there pull him out of line. Are you sure of this, Cat?"

"Yes, please."

"Okay, I'll go pick him up, but it will be over an hour before I can make it to hospital."

"What about Jenny?"

"She's taken care of. My neighbor said Jenny could stay with her until I get back."

"I'm sorry."

"Cat, it's fine. I think it's a treat for her and Jenny. Mrs. McMillan's kids are no longer at home, so it gives her a chance to relive those days. She adores Jenny. I just hope you are sure this is what you want. He hurt you before, Cat."

"Yes, I'm sure. I'll explain it later. It's complicated."

"Okay, I'll be there as soon as I can, and by the way, you owe me big-time for this one."

"Yes, love, and thanks."

"Okay then, I'll see you soon. Bye."

"Bye."

Chapter Seventeen

aitlin stared at a line in the letter: *If it were in my power, I would take you in my arms and ask you to share the rest of my life with me.* She took a deep breath and exhaled slowly. Michael still held such power over her. She continued to stare at those words as she thought about the life they were denied. Tears streamed down her face. Whatever they had done to Michael must have been unbearable, yet the young boy she had fallen madly in love with was there. He came to her through his words. That man she loved so—still loved—was older, yet he spoke to her in a way that touched her as no other man had. Caitlin thought back to that time fifteen years ago.

Caitlin had traveled to this rural South Georgia town, Roseville, in the summer of 1989. Her father, Colin, met Michael's parents, Walter and Peggy, when they visited Scotland a few years earlier. Her dad was working in a pub Walter had chosen to spend a few hours in while his wife did some shopping. Before Walter left to rejoin his wife, her dad had convinced him to go fishing the following day. Over the next few days, her dad served as Walter's fishing guide, and a friendship developed that resulted in Walter inviting Colin to come to Roseville to allow Walter a chance to show her dad what fishing across the pond was like. Her dad initially refused, but when Walter reminded him he was only doing what Scots had done for generations, sharing his home with a friend, her dad agreed.

Caitlin came as a substitute for her mum. Her mum was unable to leave her sister, who had taken ill and required constant supervision. Caitlin had traveled very little prior to this time and thought of the trip as a great adventure. She was at the top of her class in school and planned to go to university in two years, so her mum and dad said she should think of it as a nice reward for making such high marks. Michael still had three years remaining in high school, as he referred to it.

Michael was fifteen, or fifteen and nine months, as he was quick to point out the first time his age was mentioned. She was sixteen, or sixteen and five months, using Michael's descriptor for age. She had smiled at his attempt to hasten his pursuit of adulthood by measuring each passing month and suggested he should count days as well. The pained look on his face told her the barb had hit its mark.

"A child" was her first impression when she met Michael at Twin Oaks. She soon discovered he was much more. Michael was, in fact, this wonder child who would pull her in so, so deeply that she surrendered and was hopelessly lost in love.

Caitlin's first two days at Twin Oaks were uneventful. Michael's family served as their host and introduced them to several of their friends. Their accents and looks made them quite the novelty. Her red hair, green eyes, and Scottish brogue were a hit, and she was soon being invited to parties given by teenagers who were friends of Michael.

Everything changed after the pool party on the third day. She hadn't brought a swimsuit with her, so Michael's sister, Becky, had taken her to a shop earlier that morning. Later the same day, Becky drove Michael and her to the pool party being held at Kelsie's, a friend and classmate of Michael. The boys were playing a game of volleyball in the pool, and the girls were sitting beside the pool, "working on their tan," as one of the girls had observed. She was sitting by Kelsie, and they were talking.

"Isn't it funny how boys always want to show off their muscles to impress the girls? It's the same in Scotland. You would think they might have advanced beyond caveman antics."

"I guess, but Michael isn't like the others."

"What do you mean?"

"Well, don't get me wrong. He has the body, but there is more."

"More? I don't see it."

"I'll give you an example."

"Okay."

"We were in lit class this past year. Ms. Cofer, our teacher, asked each of us to write an essay about the novel we had chosen to read that grading period. She had been disappointed at our effort, so she said she would read an example to show us what we should aspire for in our next attempt. The student had read *The Great Gatsby*, and there was a line from the essay I still recall: 'Fortune in love and life is often a result of timing.' As the teacher finished reading, I was looking at Michael, and from the expression on his face, I was certain he was the one who wrote the essay. All I'm saying is his essay changed the way I thought of Michael from that day on."

"Maybe his parents helped or wrote it for him."

Kelsie smiled. "It's your loss. What I wouldn't give to have him as my chaperone."

Caitlin felt certain Kelsie was wrong and was determined to prove it. If Michael was so special, there had to be evidence. So she decided to temper her tongue and give him the opportunity to show her. It would be difficult since they were rarely alone, but there was still time. Caitlin and her dad were staying in Roseville for another week.

Later that night, during dinner, Mr. Williams announced he had arranged a trip to Florida. He and dad would be leaving early the next morning to go deep-sea fishing in the Gulf of Mexico. Caitlin was excited until Mr. Williams added Michael would also be going with them. After they finished their meal, she excused herself and went to her room. Caitlin knew she had to be patient, but she was in a state of despair. How was she going to find out the truth if Michael was gone?

While lying in bed, she decided to write her mum a letter the next day since she would have plenty of time, and it would also serve as a distraction. For the past few days, she had mailed her mum a postcard from the ones she had purchased at the London airport, Atlanta airport, and in Roseville while shopping with Becky. She thought it would be nice to give her mum a daily update. Her mum was terribly disappointed about not being able to make the trip with dad, and this was a way of sharing the experience with her. However, she couldn't stop thinking about Michael, and her last thought as she drifted off to sleep was, *Could Kelsie possibly be right?*

When Caitlin woke the next morning, the men had been gone for several hours and were not expected to return until late in the afternoon. After breakfast, Mrs. Williams asked if she would like to accompany her while she ran a few errands, but Caitlin told her she thought she was going to use the time to write a letter to her mum. Mrs. Williams said that was thoughtful and told Caitlin she would find a pen and paper on Michael's desk if she needed it. Mrs. Williams then assured Caitlin she would only be gone a little over an hour and left.

Caitlin was now alone, and after hearing the car drive away, she went upstairs to Michael's room. Walking into the room, she closed her eyes, and just stood there for a moment. The fear she had concerning Michael seemed so real as she stood there and thought back over the past few days. She then walked over to the desk and, seeing no pens or paper, looked in the drawers until she located both. Caitlin thought about going back to her room, but the old desk and chair seemed so inviting that she took a seat and began to write.

Caitlin stopped when she heard a clock chime somewhere in the house. It startled her, and she glanced over at a small clock on a bedside table. It was ten, which meant she had been writing for more than twenty minutes.

A few minutes later, Caitlin finished the letter, folded it, and put everything back in place. As she started to leave, Caitlin was drawn to the windows. *This is what Michael sees every morning*, she thought as she looked out the windows and walked over to them. She stared out at the fields and the barn beyond the yard to the white picket fence in the distance that surrounded Twin Oaks.

Watching the horses playing in the field, Caitlin wondered if Michael understood how fortunate he was. She then turned, saw an open school planner lying on the bedside table, and read what was written in the margin: *I fear I may not see my love tomorrow.*

As she continued to stare at those words, Caitlin felt something move through her. *What if there is someone else?* She had to know, but as Caitlin reached for the planner, the sound of the front door being opened startled her. She hurriedly picked up the planner and went back to her room, which was down the hall from Michael's, and put it under her pillow. She hoped it was not the men returning, but she knew something could have happened that might have changed their plans.

Caitlin found Michael's mother in the kitchen putting away the things she had purchased. She told Mrs. Williams she had finished the letter to her mum and thought she would take a nap before the men returned. Mrs. Williams told her there were leftovers and sandwiches if she wanted something to eat. Caitlin thanked her, said she would eat later and went back to her room. She thought Mrs. Williams might check on her soon, so Caitlin decided to give the planner a quick look and return it to Michael's bedroom.

Caitlin was in love after reading what Michael had written the day she arrived, and as she read the rest of the entries concerning the time she had been at Twin Oaks, Caitlin understood what Kelsie meant. Michael was more—so much more than she had realized. The last two lines were still fresh in her mind after fifteen years: *I have met my Daisy and lack the courage to act. I appear as a fool to the one I love.* He had signed it *Lost in Love.*

Michael might have lacked the courage to act, but it was Caitlin herself who was blind. She was so blind she had not noticed the young man she often dreamed of meeting standing in front of her.

Caitlin returned the planner and went back to her room. She thought back to that first day when they compared their schooling and recalled how she had insisted Michael admit Scottish schools were more demanding. He had deferred without a fight. *How could he possibly love such a fool as me?* She lay on the bed and cried herself to sleep.

Several hours later, Caitlin woke to a light tapping on the door to her room. It was Michael, and he had been given the task of waking her for dinner. She begged him to please make an excuse for her and tell the others she would join them in a few minutes. Michael said he would and then asked if there was something more he could do. Caitlin started quietly crying and turned away from him as she lay on the bed.

She was sure he was gone, but then she felt his hand gently rubbing her back. Caitlin turned and asked, "Could you please hold me?"

Michael pulled her into his arms, and Caitlin closed her eyes as she moved into his embrace. Caitlin often thought of that moment as the most special one of her life. She had met her true love.

Chapter Eighteen

I had just finished talking to Cliff about my change of plans when I noticed the young lady from the bank, Erin Frasier, walking toward me. I stood as she came near. "Where is Caitlin? I thought—" I stopped as Erin slapped me.

"That was for the crappy way you and your family treated my best friend. I couldn't do that at the bank because I need the job, and they may have fired me."

I rubbed my cheek as I stared at Erin. I knew I couldn't hit her, but I could stop her from slapping me again. "Okay, I guess I deserved that, but I must have misunderstood the man that pulled me out of line. I thought he said Caitlin wanted to see me, and so I naturally assumed she was coming to see me."

"You assumed wrong. I'm taking you to her, though I don't agree with the decision. Is that the only bag you have?"

"Yes, and I appreciate what you are doing."

"I'm doing this for Cat, just so you know."

"Understood."

I followed Erin as she led the way through the terminal and out into the parking lot. When we got to her car, I put my bag in the back seat and noticed a car seat.

"So how old is your child?"

"There you go again, making assumptions."

"Sorry."

"I just keep it in the car to discourage wankers like you."

I said nothing more. Though I had no idea what the term meant, I was certain it was no compliment. I thought it best to sit in silence as we drove through the night. Saying nothing seemed the best option since I was unaware of how much Erin knew. However, the stinging sensation I still felt in my cheek told me she knew enough to form an opinion. After about ten minutes, I decided I would try to find out why things had changed.

"How is Caitlin?"

"At the moment, I think she is fine."

"Where are we meeting?"

"Since she is in hospital, I suppose that is where it will have to be."

"I thought she was at the beach yesterday?"

"I wouldn't know about that, Mr. Williams."

"Look, I am just trying to find out about someone I care about. You are making this difficult."

"That is the idea, Mr. Williams. She is in hospital. She wanted to see you, so she called me. And now I am taking you to see her. It is not my place to tell you anything. If she chooses to, then so be it."

I glanced at my watch, which read seven thirty, and thought about the conversation I had earlier with Christy. The girls were excited about their plans to meet some friends at a park. It would be nice if life were so carefree. To be a child again.

I stared out into the darkness, trying to figure out what I was going to say to Caitlin to right the wrongs done to her, but how could I? It was impossible. When I first read the letter that Caitlin actually wrote, I wanted to rush to her side and show her the letter I had carried in my wallet for the past fourteen years and say, "This is why I never came. I thought you no longer loved me, and I never knew you were pregnant." But I couldn't. Caitlin might have been the victim as I was, but it had not been her parents that constructed the web of deceit. It was mine.

When I first read the letter I thought was from Caitlin, I was disgusted and tossed it into my desk drawer at home. I was then sentenced to military school for my part in what Mom referred to as "the mess" and, after a year, was allowed to return to Roseville High. I found the letter when I was looking for some lead for my pencil. I read it again and thought back at how devastated I had been when I first read it. That was when I decided I would use it as a reminder of how foolish I had been. I folded it up and put it in my wallet so it would always be nearby.

I knew how childish my thought of rushing to Caitlin and using the letter in an attempt to plead my innocence was, but that letter so altered what I thought was the truth concerning that portion of my life. Before I read the letter I found in the attic, I thought what happened between Caitlin and I had been a lie and was something in the distant past that had little bearing on my life other than serving as a reminder that people you fall in love with may betray that love. I now realized how wrong I had been.

"Why so quiet, Michael? Not getting nervous, are you?"

"No. I just thought it best to say nothing since anything I say seems to offend you."

"You are the smart one, and that is the smartest thing you have said tonight. And we are here."

Erin turned into a parking lot with a sign posted at the entrance that read, Hospital Parking Only.

I followed as she led the way into what looked like an emergency-room entrance and then over to a bank of elevators. Several minutes later, after navigating the labyrinth of corridors, we stopped outside a door.

"Wait here," Erin ordered as she pushed the door open and went inside.

Chapter Nineteen

I was standing outside Caitlin's door, holding my bag as I awaited the final verdict. After what seemed like an eternity, Erin opened the door and walked out. It was obvious that she had been crying.

"Is she okay?"

"This is where I leave you, but you had better not dare hurt my friend. Do you understand?"

"Yes, it was never my intention."

I watched as Erin walked away, turned at the end of the corridor, and was gone. I had wanted to thank her, but I knew it would only anger her. So instead, I said nothing. I turned back to the door and tapped lightly on it.

"Come in," a voice from inside said.

I pushed the door open and walked into the room. A lamp on a small bedside table provided the only light, but it was sufficient for me to see it was Caitlin in the bed. My first thought was, *She is more beautiful than I remembered.* I then noticed the letter beside the lamp.

"Caitlin, I'm sorry if I upset you by coming to Scotland. I just felt I needed to see you and apologize personally."

Caitlin smiled, "There's the Michael I know."

I put my bag against the wall and walked over and sat in a chair next to the bed. "Your friend is not exactly a fan of mine."

"Sorry. I'm afraid that may be my fault. She has been one of the few people I confided in, and…well, let's just say she thinks you are one of those men who promise a young girl to love her forever and then changes his mind."

"I see. That helps to explain her attitude." I had avoided the obvious question, as I was fearful of the answer. But I had to know. "Caitie, why are you in the hospital?"

"I fainted, and the doctor thought I should stay overnight. But can we talk about it later?"

"Sure."

"Michael, I must know. How could you write me that horrible letter after I came home?"

"I didn't."

"What?"

"I am fairly certain my mother intercepted all the letters we wrote each other and then sent us each the one letter instead."

"Why?"

"You read the letter. Why do you think? She wanted to destroy what we had, so she made each of us think the other had decided it was a mistake."

"I cried for weeks, Michael. I—"

"I know, Caitie. Mom is a force to reckon with, and money and power are not something to be underestimated in a small town."

"Michael, what was the letter like that you received from me?"

I almost took it out of my wallet and let her read it, but it would have been too embarrassing. She would have thought I was a fool. "It said when you got home, you realized what a mistake it all was, and you thought it was best if we both went back to the life we had before we met. You said there were just too many obstacles that would prevent us from ever being together, and you felt they would be impossible to overcome. You were also excited about going to university in a year and wished me the best."

"How…how could you believe—"

"What, Caitie?"

"How could you think I would do that to you? I was in love with you, Michael."

"I'm sorry. It also mentioned you had started dating a university student."

"I never!"

"I realize that now, Caitie. But I was a teenager at the time, and the letter was the only communication I had with you. You must understand my mom has a talent for manipulation." I thought about pointing out that she had been fooled as well by a letter from dear Mom, but I knew that would only make her feel worse.

"Michael, does your family know you are here?"

"No, only a cousin and possibly our lawyer. I can trust them, but I intend to tell my family when I return home."

"I'm not sure that would be wise."

"Caitie, I'm definitely having a conversation with Mom. She needs to understand the full extent of the damage she has done. What she did was unconscionable." I noticed I had started using Caitie, which was the name I first used after I found her crying in her room fifteen years earlier. I stood and took her hand as she started crying. "Are you okay? Do I need to call a nurse?"

"No, I'm fine," she said as she wiped the tears with a tissue.

"I thought you might be in pain."

"No, I just can't believe someone would do what she did. Before I read the letter that you gave Erin, I thought you no longer cared for me."

"That's how I felt also. When your friend told me that you didn't want to see me, I decided

I would try your parents' home, hoping I could at least see my son before I went home. Instead, I met your brother, and he told me I must have the wrong Caitlin Campbell because you had no child. I was naturally confused and concerned about what happened to our child."

Caitlin stiffened. "Michael, what specifically did you say to my brother?"

I could tell Caitie was upset but didn't understand why. "I just asked him if your child was home. Why is that so important?"

"Michael, that was our son you met."

"What?"

"Ryan is our son, but he has been raised as my brother. You can't say anything to him, promise me. You must promise me. I would die if he ever found out."

I could tell Caitie was frantic. "But, Caitie, others have to know."

"Michael, your mother isn't the only clever one. My mum pretended to be pregnant, and in the last four months of my pregnancy, I went to stay with an aunt who supposedly needed someone to care for her. She was actually in good health. Then with a grandmother who had been a midwife and a doctor who was a close friend, we were able to make it appear as if Ryan was Mum's son. Only a small number knew, and now there are only five remaining who know the truth."

"That's unbelievable."

"Yes, and I pray he never learns the truth. It would destroy me. You saw him, Michael. He was such a wonderful child, and he is such a great young man. The best part is that I was able to be a part of his life the past fourteen years."

"Did Dad know?"

"Yes, but he told my parents he would tell his wife and family that Ryan was in a good home. He said he would not tell anyone my mum and dad were raising him as their child."

I thought of pointing out that I had been denied any knowledge of the existence of my son and was now being asked to continue this deception her family had concocted, but I knew that was being selfish. My ignorance was not the result of anything Caitlin or her family had done. I was fairly certain that was the handiwork of my mom. Caitlin had lived with this secret, not being able to acknowledge the love a mother had for her son, and I couldn't imagine how difficult that must have been.

"Michael, I just wanted a normal life for Ryan. I didn't want our child to be called a bastard. Do you understand?"

"Yes, I understand, Caitie. I would never question what you did. I am just happy that Ryan is safe and with people who love him."

"He is, and when I get out of hospital tomorrow, I will introduce you to him."

"That may be awkward after my misstep."

"I think it will be okay. I'll just tell him you were mistaken about me having a child. I don't think it will be a problem. Remember, he is a teenager with a lot on his mind."

The cell phone on the bed rang, and Caitlin answered it. "Hello."

"Hello, dear?"

"Oh, hi, Mum."

"I was just calling to check on you before I go to bed."

"I'm doing fine, Mum."

"What are the plans for tomorrow?"

"Dr. Morrison is hoping he can move the MRI up rather than wait until its originally scheduled time next week, but we both know that's not likely."

"Yes."

"Mum, I think it would be best if everyone returns to a normal schedule tomorrow."

"Okay."

"Yes. I think Ryan should go to school, and Dad to work. I feel fine."

"Okay. I guess I'll see you tomorrow morning and bring you back here after you are released."

"Mum, that won't be necessary. A friend is here and has agreed to take care of that."

"Okay."

"Get some sleep, and I'll see you tomorrow after they release me."

"That's good. Just call me in the morning. Things can change."

"Yes. Get some rest. Love you, Mum."

"Love you too."

I smiled at Caitlin. "So I get to see your mom tomorrow. She may be a little surprised when she sees who your friend is."

"I thought I would tell her in the morning when we talk. It should give her time to get over the shock."

"I hope."

"Michael, I could call Erin. I'm sure she would take me home if it's a problem."

"No, it's fine. I owe your mom and dad an apology as well. It might be good to try to change the opinion they most likely have of me. Though I must admit, I will be a little more cautious after my experience with your friend Erin. She has made me a little gun-shy."

"I'm not sure Mum will be any easier."

"Maybe not quite as fiery."

"Yes, Erin can be quite the diva."

"I think it will be fine. Now, Caitie, what is the medical issue? Erin wasn't very informative."

"Promise not to worry."

Those words weren't very comforting, but I still found it hard to believe it could be anything serious. She seemed so full of life. "I'll try."

"I blacked out a few weeks ago while I was riding my bike, and the doctor had some x-rays taken. And, well, it seems I have a brain tumor."

The shock of what Caitie had said made me question what I'd just heard. "Brain tumor?"

"Yes, but Dr. Morrison seems to think it is most likely the type that can be successfully treated."

"Okay," I managed as I was reeling. I stood, took Caitlin's hands, and pulled her into my arms. "I'm so sorry, Caitie. So sorry," I repeated as I held her. I didn't know what I expected her problem to be, but it wasn't this. Then I remembered something that didn't seem right. I released her and sat back in the chair. "But, Caitie, if it was a few weeks ago, why are you still in a hospital? I thought your neighbor said you were all at the beach yesterday. Did he get it wrong?"

"No. A few weeks ago, I found out about the tumor and told Mum and Dad. I was released from hospital the next day, and we decided to get away for a day with Ryan as a treat when we had the chance. I had another episode this morning, and Dr. Morrison thought it would be best if I stayed in hospital overnight once again as a precaution. He was also going to try to get the MRI moved up, but I'm not sure that's possible. There is always a wait. The NHS, you know."

"What was the last episode like?"

"I was in my room at Mum and Dad's. I had just finished getting dressed for work when Ryan came to tell me Mum had breakfast ready. As we were walking out of my room, I passed out, and they called emergency services."

"That is scary."

"Yes, I know. Dr. Morrison suggested I take a few days off."

"Are you going to need surgery?"

"I think it depends on what they find when I have the biopsy. Dr. Morrison was hopeful that it would be benign, and radiation may be all that is required."

"That sounds optimistic. How do you feel about Dr. Morrison?"

"He seems knowledgeable enough, and the nurses all have high regard for him. Why do you ask?"

"Just concerned, Caitie."

"He did refer me to a specialist, and I see him next week."

"That sounds good."

"That's enough questions. Michael, I'm tired of lying in this bed. Let's take a walk."

"Are you sure it's okay?"

"The nurse said it was fine as long as I had someone with me."

"Okay, then let's take a walk."

Caitie pulled back the sheet that covered her legs, turned so she could sit on the edge of the bed, and slipped on her shoes. As she stood, I took her hands and moved closer. Caitie pulled me into an embrace for a moment.

"Thank you for coming, Michael."

As I looked into her eyes, I did what felt natural. I kissed Caitie, and for a moment, I was once again in the distant past, in that summer I fell hopelessly in love with her.

Chapter Twenty

Caitlin picked up her phone, went to recent calls, and selected Kathleen Campbell. Her mother answered after the first ring.

"Hello, are you okay, dear?"

"I'm fine, Mum. I just wanted to let you know we will be leaving a little after twelve."

"Okay, I was starting to get concerned."

"The doctor was a little late, but they should be done with the paperwork soon."

"Okay."

"Listen, Mum. Michael will be with me."

"Michael?"

"Yes, Michael Williams."

"I thought he went home. And why is he coming here?"

"It's complicated. He came to hospital last night, and we had a long talk. Until a few days ago, he had no idea he had a son."

"Oh my, does his mum know he is here?"

"No, but Michael said he was going to have a talk with her when he gets home."

"I might like to see that."

"I'm sure. Mum, we will see you soon. Remember to be nice!"

"I'll try."

"Love you, Mum."

"Love you too."

Forty minutes later, Caitie and I arrived at the Campbell house. I followed her with the bags as she lightly tapped on the door, opened it, and walked in.

"Mum, we're here!" Caitie shouted.

I sat the bags against the wall as a woman, I assumed was Caitie's mom, walked down the staircase.

"Mum, this is Michael."

"It is nice to finally meet you, Michael."

"It's nice to meet you as well, Mrs. Campbell."

"Kathleen, please."

"Yes, ma'am."

"Mum, Michael is taking me out for a late lunch."

"Caitlin, it is almost one, and there is food left from the lunch I made earlier."

"As I said, Michael and I are going to lunch, so I need to freshen up. Promise me you will be on your best behavior and entertain Michael while I shower and change."

"I'll try, dear."

"Thanks, Mum." She then kissed Kathleen on the cheek and went up the stairs.

Kathleen turned to me and asked, "Would you care for some tea, Michael?"

"Yes, thanks."

"Follow me," Kathleen said as she led me past the stairway to the rear of the house and into a small kitchen. "It'll just take a minute, so please take a seat. If I know my daughter, we have plenty of time."

I took a seat and watched as Kathleen filled a teakettle with water and put it on the stove. As I sat at the small table, I could envision the family sitting there at the end of the day, talking, as Kathleen prepared their meal. I was reminded of something my grandmother once said: "The kitchen is the heart of a home," and I was sure this rang true in the Campbell home.

"I have to say, Michael, when Caitlin said you were coming with her, I was a bit surprised."

"I'm sure you were, and after all I've learned the past few weeks, I can understand why. The only thing I can say in my defense is that I would hope things would have turned out differently had I known about our child."

"I would hope so, and I was shocked to hear that your parents never told you about Ryan."

Kathleen just stood there, and I could tell she wanted to say more but, instead, just shook her head.

"He is such a good lad, Michael. We are so proud of him. He is a great student and one of the best football players for his age and so tall! I think we know where he gets that from. Were you aware your dad came to see him?"

"Yes, my cousin told me a few days ago."

"Strange how time passes. It has been almost ten years. Oh my, your dad thought Ryan was the most beautiful child he had ever seen."

"Did he say why Mom didn't come?"

"Your dad told Colin she thought it was best not to see the child."

"That sounds like Mom. It was probably good she didn't come."

"Your dad enjoyed it so much that he stayed longer than he planned. We took Ryan to a park on one of those days. I'll never forget your dad laughing at Ryan eating ice cream."

"Ice cream?"

"Yes, Walter bought him a cup of ice cream, and when he finished, I don't think there was anywhere on the child that wasn't sticky."

"Kids can be messy."

"Yes, they can," Kathleen said as she smiled. "Michael, Colin and I thought a lot of your dad, and we were sad to hear of his death."

"Yes, I still find it hard to believe he is gone at times."

"Colin and I thought of your dad as family."

"What about Mom?"

"I think it is best not to say. I met her only once when she and Walter came to Scotland after they learned our Caitlin was expecting. I guess I would have to say she was protective, if I were being nice."

"That's probably being too nice, but why do you say that?"

"I'll tell you, Michael, since Caitlin mentioned you were going to have a talk with your mother about everything when you get home. I think you should know what went on at that meeting. In fact, I think you should have been told about the child back then, but please don't mention any of this to Caitlin. She doesn't need to have this on her mind as she deals with what she is facing."

"I agree."

"They never said anything to you about Ryan?"

"No."

"That is hard to understand."

"Not if you lived with my mom, but you were going to tell me about the time my parents came over."

"Yes, like I said, they came over after learning Caitlin was pregnant. Your mother called from the hotel where they were staying and asked if we—just Colin and I—could meet them in their hotel room. So we go there, and after we talked with them for a few minutes, I asked where you were. Peggy told us you were not going to be involved in the matter. She then said, 'Kathleen, the four of us will be the ones who come up with a solution to this problem.'"

"Problem?"

"Yes, and then she mentioned that she knew of doctors in the States who our Caitlin could see and have a procedure. At this point, Colin got mad and said he didn't want to hear of such talk. He would not allow it."

"Good for him."

"I think your mother realized abortion was not going to be considered as an option. That was when she asked if we could make it clear to Caitlin that she should not try to make any further contact with you. She then said she would make sure you wrote Caitlin a letter. Peggy—"

I interrupted, "But I wrote two before I got Caitlin's letter."

"Caitlin only received one letter, Michael, and it so upset her!"

I could see the pain the memory of that letter still caused after all these years, as Kathleen wiped the tears from her eyes.

"A person should think about the harm they may cause before they write such. Colin and I were concerned for weeks about—"

"Kathleen, I didn't write that letter."

"What?"

"Mom sent both of us letters. Mine was similar to Caitlin's, and it still upsets me as well when I think about how it impacted my life."

"Why would she do that?"

"Because…" I stopped for a moment, as I realized the rage building within me had resulted in my raising my voice to the point where it startled Kathleen. "I'm sorry. It's just that there are times when Mom is a little more than I can take."

"What were you going to say?"

"Because she wanted to be sure it was over."

"I should have known."

"How?"

"Because of her insistence that Caitlin stop writing you."

"She has been known to be persistent."

"And then she threatened Caitlin if—"

"Threatened? What do you mean?"

"Well, she never actually said she was going to do it, but she said it could be done."

"Kathleen, I don't understand. What did Mom say she might do?"

"Rape, Michael. She said our Caitlin could be charged with rape."

"My god, what was she thinking?"

"Michael, I think your mother was just trying to protect you."

"Kathleen, what exactly did she say?"

"She said she had talked with her lawyer, and he told her the age of consent in Georgia at the time you and Caitlin were together was sixteen. Since Caitlin was sixteen and you were still fifteen, it would legally be considered rape."

"I can't believe that. What did Dad say?"

"He told us there wouldn't be any charges filed against Caitlin, and he even told your mum he thought they had agreed not to bring that up."

"Mom has a mind of her own, and I think Dad should have realized she would use it if she thought it was necessary."

"Like I said, Michael, I think your mother wanted to protect you, and she was probably worried the scandal would ruin your life. She was desperate."

"That doesn't excuse the things she said. Kathleen, what was decided?"

"Nothing the first day. I told your parents that Colin and I needed some time to consider things, and we would meet with them again the next morning. I could see this didn't please Peggy, but she agreed. On the way home, I told Colin we were going to have to raise the child, and he agreed. I sensed your mother was not going to allow you and Caitlin to be together under any circumstances. The next day, we told them what we had decided."

"What was their reaction?"

"Your mother seemed relieved."

"And Dad?"

"He insisted they should at least help with the expenses, and he said he would talk with Colin about it later."

"And that's all?"

"Michael, Colin and I didn't really want to be around your parents after the way Peggy acted that first day. We were just ready for it to be over."

"I can understand. What was Caitlin's reaction?"

"We never told her the details, just that we were going to raise the child. She was already terribly upset, and then your letter came. Colin and I were worried. A person can only take so much."

"I think it was wise." It was very humbling to watch as Kathleen went back to the stove, poured two cups of tea, and then brought the cups to the table on a small tray. After all the pain my family had caused, she was treating me as a welcomed guest in her home. She should hate me, and how could my mother be so cruel?

"You may want to let it cool for a bit, and there is sugar and milk on the table."

"Thank you," I said as I took the lid off the sugar bowl, put two small spoonfuls of sugar in my cup, and stirred it gently. "Did Caitlin say anything to my father about me when he came to see Ryan?"

"Caitlin never saw your dad, Michael."

"Why?"

"Caitlin was doing so much better at the time. She was working at the bank, enjoying the time with Ryan, and had started going out occasionally with some girls from work. Colin and I were worried that seeing your father might upset her, so Colin told Walter it would be best if he just saw Ryan. It was simple; Walter would see Ryan while Caitlin was working."

I was struggling to understand how life could be so unfair. I was at a loss for what to say.

"Michael, please don't hurt Caitlin. I was so worried when she told me this morning that you were with her."

I could sense the concern in Kathleen's voice. I knew I should stop thinking about things I couldn't change and focus on what I could do to ease a parent's distress. "It was never my intention to hurt anyone by coming to Scotland, especially Caitlin. I think I would feel the same way, though, if I were in your place. I just felt I needed to see her and apologize to all of you for what my family did."

"Thank you, Michael. A parent always worries about their children."

"Yes, they do."

"Do you have kids, Michael? I mean, other than Ryan?"

"Yes, two girls, a five-year-old and a three-year-old."

"They are so precious at that age. Cherish the time with them. They will be teenagers before you realize it."

"I try."

"Colin and I asked Caitlin to move back in after she fainted that first time. She lived with us when Ryan was little, but she moved into a flat after Ryan started school. She was promoted at the bank, and it just didn't look right, still living at home with Mum and Dad. Our girl is so smart, Michael. Did you know she was going to uni before…?"

"Yes, she said something about it when she visited Twin Oaks that summer."

"She didn't go, but she took some banking courses after she worked at the bank for a few years. And she did so well they promoted her."

"I'm sure you both are proud of her."

"Yes, we are. You know, the funny thing is, I think Caitlin was happy when we told her we thought it was best if she moved back in with us."

I smiled as I looked across the table at Kathleen. I was so thankful Ryan had been able to grow up in a home where he was loved. "I think that was wise, and I'm sure she enjoys the extra time with Ryan."

"Yes, that girl does think the sun rises and sets on the lad."

I was reminded of those early years with Becky and the irony of life. "I had a sister who was much older than me, and I didn't realize how special she was until I was older."

"Michael, I think love is something we all need a good dose of when we are little, and I would like to think Ryan got an extra dose."

I was about to agree with Kathleen when I heard the patter of footsteps coming down the stairs. I turned to see Caitlin coming toward me. "Wow, you do clean up good."

"Not exactly the response I expected. Have you two been plotting?" she asked.

"No, dear, we just had a good talk over some tea. Michael, I want to thank you for being so patient in listening to an old lady."

"My pleasure. I enjoyed it, and you shouldn't say that about yourself. When I saw you coming down the stairs earlier, I almost asked Caitlin if she had a sister."

"You are quite the charmer, and I will take that as a compliment. I enjoyed our little talk as well. It is a shame we didn't have it earlier."

"Yes, I would have liked that."

"Ready?" Caitlin asked as she smiled at me.

"Sure," I said as I stood facing Katherine, then continued, "Thank you for welcoming me into your home, and I am very appreciative of everything you have done for Ryan."

"We try our best," Kathleen said as she stood, walked around the table, and pulled Caitlin close. She then kissed her and whispered, "Hold fast to your heart, dear."

"Love you too, Mum."

Chapter Twenty-One

It was chilly and misting rain, so Caitie asked to be seated inside with a view across the city skyline stretching out to the sea. As I looked across the table, I thought of what Mom would say if she saw the two of us together and how angry she would be if she knew what I was thinking as I smiled at Caitie.

"Are you happy?" I asked.

Caitie flushed a puzzled smile. "I'm not sure I understand."

"You get freshened up, change into this fabulous dress, and I haven't showered or shaved in over a day and am still wearing the clothes I slept in."

Caitie smiled again. "I like the rugged look. It sort of goes with the Scottish life."

"Well, I have to agree the weather here does favor the hardy."

"Honestly, Michael, people probably think you're some American cowboy who was lucky enough to get himself a date with a bonnie Scottish lass."

"More like some homeless American you took pity on."

"There is that," Caitie said as she laughed.

"What did your mom say to you before we left?"

"Oh, I can't. Mum/daughter secrets are off-limits."

I smiled and reached across the table and squeezed her hand. The first few months after learning of Christy's affair had been difficult, and even now, they had their moments. I loved Christy, but if I were being honest, the love I had felt for Caitie was so much more. That feeling was returning. Though

I knew most would discount it as teenage infatuation, I felt it even now as I sat with her. There was something about Caitie that I found so enchanting. There was something beyond the engaging banter and spontaneity that said, "Come with me and live life fully." This intangible was pulling me ever…

"Michael, are you listening?"

"What? No, I'm sorry. What did you say?"

"I've changed my mind. I think I would rather get something to eat at a pub. This is nice, but I want some proper food. Let me take you somewhere else."

"Lead the way. I just want you to be happy."

"Do you now?" Caitie said as she smiled.

The next four hours were a blur as we ate at a pub that she often frequented, took a walk up to the castle on the royal mile, and then went to a small club where we listened to music and enjoyed some wine. It was only a little after seven, but I thought it was time to call it a night when I saw her yawning.

"Caitie, we stayed up a little late last night, talking, and you need to get some rest. So I'm taking you home now."

"I admit I am tired, but I hate for the night to end. However, if we leave now, you can meet Ryan before he goes to bed."

"Are you sure that would be wise?"

"Yes. He loves reading about the States, so I will introduce him to an actual American."

"Okay."

Thirty minutes later, we walked into her parents' home.

"Mum, we're back," she called out.

"I'm in the back, dear. I was making some cookies, and I was about to take them out of the oven. Come on back."

Caitie and I went through to the kitchen and sat at the table. I soon heard footsteps coming down the stairs.

"Ryan has been studying, but he has a nose for treats," Kathleen said with a wink.

"Can't say I blame him," I said.

I stood as Ryan entered. "Sorry about my mistake the other day. Right Caitlin, wrong information."

"No problem. Mum told me that Dad and Caitlin went to America to visit your family before I was born."

"Yes, I think my dad and your dad hit it off when my parents came over to Scotland a few years before that. My dad invited him to come visit us."

"I wish I could be that lucky."

"You never know."

"You live in Georgia, right?"

"Yes."

"Where did you go to school, Mr. Williams?"

"I went to a junior college in Tifton, Georgia, called ABAC for a year, and then transferred to the University of Georgia."

"The University of Georgia. Wow, I bet that place is amazing."

"Not the word I usually associate with the time I spent there, but yes, I guess, looking back, it was."

Kathleen set a platter of cookies on the table. "Okay, they are hot, so be warned."

We sat there for several minutes, eating cookies and talking. At first, I just enjoyed watching the three of them, and then my eyes settled on Ryan. I had this compelling urge to stand up, walk around the table, and hug my son. I knew this was insane for, in one moment, I could jeopardize the wonderful life Caitie and her family had worked so hard to create. My dilemma was only fair since I was able to experience, for a few brief moments, the pain Caitie had endured the past fifteen years. Then I saw Caitie yawning again. "I'll get out of here and let you get some rest." I stood, and as I did, Caitie stood also.

"I'll walk up front and wait with you until the taxi arrives."

"Michael, we have a room," Kathleen offered.

"Thanks, but I've already booked a room. I'll be back tomorrow before I leave."

"It was nice meeting you, Mr. Williams," Ryan said.

"It was nice meeting you as well, Ryan, and when I get home, I'll send you a UGA hat. That is if it is okay with Mom."

Ryan looked at Kathleen. "Is it okay, Mum?"

"Sure, and thank you, Michael."

Caitie and I walked back to the living room and sat on the sofa. I called a taxi and was told it should arrive in about fifteen minutes.

Caitie stretched out and rested her head in my lap. "Could you please rub my back, Michael?"

"Yes." And as I drew circles on her back, she smiled and relaxed. I realized I was falling in love again, something I had not expected. This beautiful, caring young woman was taking hold of my heart once again, and a love I thought had been lost forever was growing even stronger each moment.

Chapter Twenty-Two

As I stood on the balcony and stared into the distance, I made a futile attempt to locate the general area where I had been a few hours earlier. Hopefully, Caitie was now asleep and resting. It was difficult to say no to her mom's request to stay with them for the night, but it would have been even more difficult to have accepted the offer. So near yet so far.

I worried about the effect our venture out on the town might have on Caitie. It was not that it was too strenuous, but she had already suffered two episodes. The thought that I might be the cause of a third was concerning. As I stepped back to close the sliding door that led into the room, I heard a knock at my door. Probably just a mistake. But as I started closing the door, a second series of taps began.

"Just a minute. I was outside!" I shouted, hoping they could hear me. When I opened the door, I saw Caitie standing in the corridor, and before I could say anything, she stepped through the doorway and pulled me into an embrace.

"Please hold me," Caitie managed through the tears. "I thought you were gone."

"Caitie, I'm sorry. I was just outside." I pushed the door closed as I held her. How can my life ever be the same? To Caitie, I said, "I told you I would see you tomorrow before I leave. How did you get to the hotel?"

"Taxi. I didn't think I could ask anyone, and I knew you would be angry if I drove. I just couldn't sleep knowing you were leaving tomorrow. I had to be with you, Michael. I know I should be ashamed, but I'm not."

As we held each other, a thought came to me: *Once again, she is the brave one, willing to bare her innermost feelings.*

Caitie released me and walked toward the balcony. "It is beautiful. Edinburgh at night."

"Yes, she is. I was just admiring the view myself, but I have to confess I was more concerned with locating a particular place."

Caitie returned to me and kissed me. "I brought you something."

"Okay?"

"It's a picture of Ryan," she answered as she took a photo from her pocket.

"Thanks. I'll put it in my office at work."

"It won't cause a problem, will it?"

"I don't see how it would. I'll just say he is the son of a close friend who lives in Scotland."

"I keep a picture of him on my desk at work. If I am having a rough day, it reminds me how fortunate I am to be a part of his life."

"It is hard for me to imagine my girls being his age."

"*Tempus fugit.* It does pass so quickly."

"That has been a recurring thought of mine the past few days, Caitie."

Caitie took my hand and led me back onto the balcony.

"I'm not sure how long we will be able to tolerate the chilly air. It is a little different from Roseville."

"Michael, you are looking at it from the wrong perspective. This is the reason we Scots are so close. The elements bind us," Caitie said as she moved beside me and put her arms around me.

"There is that," I observed. As we stood there, looking across the city gradually growing darker, an internal clock was ticking down the time I had remaining with Caitie—a clock I would do almost anything to stop. Yet I knew it was impossible to do so.

I remembered similar experiences I had as a child when it was near the end of a vacation. The last day was always the most miserable because all I could think about was that tomorrow the vacation was over, and everyone would return to their normal routine back at home. Somehow, I had to make sure this was not the last day I shared with Caitie.

I pulled her close. "Stay with me tonight, Caitie. I don't think I could sleep knowing you were somewhere out there. So close yet not with me."

Chapter Twenty-Three

I woke to the vibrating of my watch and reached for Caitie. I turned and saw a note on the pillow she had used. *She's gone*, I thought as I set up and opened the note.

Dearest Michael,

I woke this morning at sunrise and watched you as you slept. It is strange how something so ordinary can seem so special. I held you for a moment, and as I kissed you lightly on your cheek, a terrible thought came to me: this may be the last time I kiss you as my love. I then dressed and sat in a chair near the bed to watch you as I wrote this letter.

I know when you leave in a few hours it will most likely be the last time I see you, for we seem compelled to live separate lives. Though fate has been so unfair, we can at least take comfort with the memories we have. I will always cherish those.

I'm sorry I didn't have the courage to wait for you to wake, my love. It would have been too painful to face you and say what must be said knowing you would be leaving in a few hours.

Michael, I find it unbearable to put on paper what I have to say to you, but I must. The family you have is what I imagined ours would have been like if we had married and shared a life together with Ryan. A family that cre-ates wonderful memories as they grow old together. Michael, a family like that is precious. Cherish what you have and hold fast to it.

I do have a confession to make. I took the shirt you loaned me to sleep in last night. I hope you can forgive me, for I feel on those nights when I am troubled or not feeling well, it will give me comfort and remind me of how fortunate I have been in this life.

I promise to do my best to play the role of a dear friend when I see you later today but do forgive me if I kiss a dear friend goodbye.

Love,
Caitie

I could see where the tears had fallen on the note. I knew how hard it was for Caitie not to fight to stay with me, for I faced the same internal conflict. I was willing to endure the sacrifice without a fight because of the pain it would cause, and I was sure the same was true for Caitie. The destruction of two families was a steep price to pay for love—too steep.

I placed the note under my wallet so I would be sure to pack it in my bag. As I stood and started to the bathroom, I stopped and pulled back the drapes to look across the city. Edinburgh was waking, so I took a moment to look at the city that would always hold a special place for Caitie and me, the city where our love was reborn.

It was six forty-five, and I knew I needed to get moving. Ryan had to be at school at eight forty. There was a fifteen-minute taxi ride when traffic was light, and there wasn't much chance of that at this hour. I took a shower, got dressed, and packed my bag. I smiled as I placed my three remaining shirts in my bag.

After I checked to make sure I had not missed anything, I called a taxi and started out of the room. As I rode the elevator down to the lobby, a thought occurred to me: *What would Caitie think if she knew about Nicole?*

Chapter Twenty-Four

I asked the driver to send a cab back to Hill View Drive in twenty minutes. I then walked to the front door and knocked. The sound of footsteps told me I had been heard.

Ryan opened the door. "Come in, Mr. Williams. We're in the back, talking."

"Thanks. I just dropped by to say goodbye and to see Caitlin before I left." I then followed Ryan to the kitchen.

"Michael, would you like some coffee?" Kathleen asked.

"No, thanks. I'm good. I just wanted to say thank you for your hospitality and speak with Caitlin for a moment."

"You are welcome, Michael, and I hope you have a safe trip."

"Thanks, and I won't forget that hat I promised you, Ryan."

"Thanks, Mr. Williams, and it was nice meeting you."

"It was nice meeting you as well, Ryan."

I turned to Caitie. "Can we talk?"

"Sure, let's go to the living room."

I was somewhat surprised at how composed Caitie was. As I followed her back through the house, I struggled to think of what I would say to her. Caitie turned into the same room we had used the previous night and took a seat on the sofa. She motioned for me to sit beside her. I sat down, took Caitie into my arms, and kissed her. I sensed a coolness and reserve that had been absent a few hours earlier, which told me something had changed. "Are your parents upset about last night?"

"Not really. Mum is the only one that knows, and all she said was, 'You are an adult now, young lady, and my days of trying to make decisions for you are over.'"

I looked into her eyes—those bright, radiant green eyes that seemed to shimmer in the light. Those same eyes had pulled me in so deeply when we first met. "Did she remind you I had a family?"

"That came up."

"Remind her that I was the one who asked you to stay, Caitie, and I'm not sure I would be able to leave today if you hadn't stayed."

"I love you, Michael. How could I say no?"

"And I love you, but I'm returning to my family today. So maybe that will ease your mother's worries."

"Maybe?" Caitie was gently caressing my hand as she looked down. "Michael, I…even now, I wish I could run away with you, and…" She stopped and looked up at me with tears in her eyes. "I'm sorry…" She stopped again, overwhelmed with emotion, wiped the tears from her eyes, and looked back down at her hands.

"Caitie, I'm going to call occasionally to check on how you are doing." She said nothing for a moment, and I thought she was weighing the impact of what I had suggested.

"No," Catie whispered softly as she continued to look down.

"Caitie, I don't understand. What do you mean?"

"We can't continue. I can't be party to such lies and deceit."

"Do you realize how hard this will be on…" I stopped because the look she gave me was humiliating. I realized how I sounded. Once again, she was being the brave one, and she was asking me to stand with her. "I understand. I will do whatever you ask, Caitie, but I'm very concerned about your health. I can't just leave not knowing."

"I will have Mum or Dad call you to let you know how things are going. I think it will be better that way."

"Okay. Can I at least write you?"

"Yes…"

I thought, *At least I have that*, and then she continued.

"Only, and I do mean only, if the letters can be read by any of my family. I am tired of the deceit. Just write like you were keeping a journal. Write about your life, kids, and the family. But I only want you to write me once a year for my birthday.

Those words were devastating, but I knew I had no choice. "Okay."

"But, Michael, I can't write you."

"What?"

"Michael, there is no risk if your letter is read by someone other than me, but a letter from me to you is a different matter. Why is a woman in Scotland writing my husband? It is wrong, Michael, and like I said, the deceit needs to stop. I lost my son, remember."

"Yes, I understand. Caitie, do you regret staying with me last night?"

She looked at me and smiled, "I will always love you and will always cherish that night. No, it was our chance to share what we should have had a lifetime of...our love."

It was hard to describe what I felt. It was like a calm slowly replacing the turmoil within me as I processed all that Caitie had said. I knew she was right. For a moment, we were quiet, and I could hear Ryan and Kathleen talking in the kitchen. How strange it was. Life does move on, and we each must respond to the change it brings.

"Michael, I think it would be best if you said nothing to your wife."

"I was, but now I'm not so sure. I think it may be best to just have a talk with my mom."

"Michael, you don't have to do that for me."

"Caitie, I know I don't have to, but you have suffered in silence and me, in ignorance, for too long. Someone needs to say something to her about what she did to us."

"I worry it will only cause more harm."

"I won't say anything that would affect Ryan." I then heard a car horn. "I guess that is my ride. Caitie, I will always love you."

We both stood, and for a moment, I looked into her eyes for what I feared would be the last time, then I kissed her.

Caitie took a small tissue and wiped her eyes. "I can't stand outside and watch you leave. I just can't, Michael. Please understand."

"I do, Caitie." I took the note I had written from my pocket and handed it to her. "I found your note, so I thought I would write you one. Tell Ryan and your mom goodbye for me."

We kissed, and I walked to the door. Just before leaving, I turned and looked at her sitting on the couch. I smiled, and she struggled but smiled back at me. That was the last image I had of Caitie.

Chapter Twenty-Five

It was a fifteen-minute ride to the pub in Old Town in which Colin was a part owner. I paid the driver as the cab stopped in front of the pub.

"Could you please wait until I check to see if the man I'm looking for is here?"

"Yes."

"Also, could you pick me up in front of the pub in thirty minutes? I'll make it worth your while."

"I'll try, but if something comes up, I'll send a mate."

"Fine. Just hit the horn if I'm not waiting out front."

"Okay."

I glanced at my watch. I knew the pub didn't open until ten thirty, and that was almost an hour from now. I tried the door but found it was locked, so I tapped on the door.

"We open in about an hour!" a voice from inside shouted.

"Sorry, but I need to talk to Colin Campbell."

A short time later, I heard footsteps approaching the door. "And just what might you be needing to speak to Colin about?" a voice from behind the door asked.

The highland brogue that was distinctive even in his family brought a smile to my face, as I remembered the first time that I had heard it fifteen years ago. "I just wanted to tell him hello from the Williams family."

I could hear the locks being turned, and soon the door opened. Colin stood in front of me. Though he had changed some, it was not enough to keep me from recognizing him.

"And just who might you be?"

"Michael, Michael Williams. Walter's son."

"Aye. Caitlin and Kathleen told me you were in town. I missed you when you came to the house. Come in. Come in, lad."

I waved at the cab, and he pulled away as I stepped down into the pub and followed Colin. He walked behind the bar.

"Take a seat. We will raise a glass to Walter," Colin said as he reached to the back of a vast array of bottles that lined the mirrored back wall of the bar and selected a bottle. "Now I bet you ne'er tried this one."

I could tell Colin was in his element. I could imagine him working the bar, peppering his patrons with lively banter that kept them engaged, and I was sure it didn't hurt the bottom line. I looked at the label of the bottle Colin had selected. "Can't say I've heard of it."

"Your dad and I drank a toast at a pub over fifteen years ago with a wee bit of this. It was before I went to visit Walter. The next day, we went fishing and had a great time. He told me he had promised his grandfather that he would come to Scotland one day."

"Yes, his grandfather was a Murray. Though he never visited Scotland himself, he told my father stories that he remembered hearing as a child. Stories about the beauty of the land and the people who were his ancestors. Dad always planned to take his grandfather with him when he made the trip. Unfortunately, his grandfather died when Dad was in his last year of college."

"Michael, he was a special man, that father of yours."

"Yes, I have found that I miss him even more as I get older."

Colin was quiet for a moment as he set two glasses on the bar. "Kathleen told me about the talk she had with you. We always knew something wasn't right."

"Yes, I would have to say that was not my family at its best."

"To be honest, Michael, it was a hard time for all, and things were said and done that might be best to leave in the past."

"I think you are being truly kind, Mr. Campbell. Your family has made great sacrifices to give Ryan a normal life. On the other hand, my family has made little or no sacrifice. It seems so unjust."

"I think you may be a bit harsh, Michael. Your dad insisted he be allowed to send money each month to help with expenses, and we have put it in the bank for Ryan to use when he goes to university."

"I was unaware he did that, but it is still such a small thing when compared to what your family has done."

"Michael, Walter saw you as the man who would, one day, oversee this great company he had built. He saw you as the man who would take care of this company and pass it down to the next generation. He may not have agreed with your mum on everything, but I'm sure—"

I interrupted Colin, "What do you mean about him not agreeing with Mom?"

"When Walter came by himself to see Ryan, he told me he didn't agree with some of the things your mum said. And he—"

This was frustrating, but I was determined to get specifics as I interrupted again, "What part did he not agree with Mom on?"

"Most of it… Not keeping the baby, saying our Caitlin took advantage, and not telling you about Ryan. Walter told me that before he saw how happy Ryan was, he had made up his mind to tell you. But after he saw Ryan, he said he weren't so sure anymore." Colin paused for a moment and poured a drink for us into the two glasses then continued, "I told Walter it may be best to leave things be."

I looked at Colin, who seemed to straighten up as if he took pride in the pronouncement he had just made.

"Did Caitlin or Kathleen know about this?"

"No, they didn't. Walter and I talked it over while we were fishing. He asked me to say nothing until he decided, and then he had a heart attack." Colin took a sip of his drink and continued, "So a wee bit later, he calls me and says he thinks I was right, and it was probably best to leave things as they be."

My mind was in turmoil, and I could only imagine what the impact on Caitie would be if she became aware of this revelation. This occurred at least a year before I met Christy. We had a chance for a life together, yet I was sure that even if Dad had made the decision to tell me, Mom would have intervened.

There were so many opportunities all dashed by our parents, who thought they knew best. Why had I not...? Then I remembered the letter. The letter I still carried in my wallet. The letter I had not shown Caitie. How could I?

"You needn't worry, Michael. I kept my word. No one else has heard this from my lips and ne'er will. I owed that to Walter."

"I think it might be best."

Colin raised his drink. "To Walter, a good man."

I raised my glass and took a sip. It was not like the harsh whiskey I was more accustomed to but was rather smooth with a hint of sweetness. "Very good."

"It's called Auchentoshan. That is Scottish for 'corner of the field.' This particular bottle is the Auchentoshan 21."

"It's not like most of the whiskeys I've had."

"It's a bit on the sweet side, but I am fond of it."

For the second time today, I heard a horn signaling an end to a special moment with someone.

"That is my ride, I believe. I can never express in words how grateful I am for all you and your family have done for Ryan," I said as I reached in my pocket and took out an envelope. "Please use this if there is ever anything Ryan needs. If it isn't needed for that purpose, use it to take the family on a vacation."

Colin held his hands up as if not wanting to touch the envelope. "No, Michael, I can't take that. We are doing fine, and I think you can tell Ryan is doing great. We still get the money from your family each month, so no."

"I know that, but it would make me feel better. Please let a father do this for his son, Mr. Campbell."

"Fine," Colin said, and then he raised his glass and continued, "*Lang may yer lum reek.*"

We both finished our drinks.

"It means, 'I wish you well in the future,'" Colin said, and then he came around the bar, took my hand, and pulled me into a hug. "I'm starting to see a wee bit of Walter in you."

"Thank you, sir, and I wish you well too. Take care and I apologize if I interfered with your daily routine."

"Not to worry, and maybe if you come back, we may try a wee bit of fishing one day."

"That sounds inviting."

As I walked back to the entrance, Colin followed me until I reached the door. He then unlocked the door and closed it after I walked out. The sound of the locks being reset brought a thought to mind: *How many doors have I closed on my past in the last few hours?*

As I took a seat in the back of the taxi, I saw a familiar face. "Thanks for coming back for me."

"No problem, sir. I hope I gave you enough time."

"Yes, thank you."

"Is it to the airport, sir?"

"Yes, it is."

"Well, I do hope you enjoyed your stay in Edinburgh."

I said nothing more. I was not in the mood for small talk. I saw the driver glance at me in the mirror and realized if I didn't say something, he would most likely start again. "Sorry, I'm just trying to organize my thoughts. I have an important meeting."

"No, that is fine, sir. I'll leave you to your thoughts then."

"Thanks." I knew the tip I gave him would more than compensate him for my reticence. I just wanted to be alone...alone with my thoughts for a time.

Chapter Twenty-Six

I retraced the route I had taken coming to Scotland. First, I flew to London and then caught a connecting flight to Atlanta that departed at one o'clock. Thankfully, Colin's potion worked its magic, and I slept through most of the flight to Atlanta. It was almost five when I retrieved my truck from long-term parking and started for Murphy. Traffic was lighter than I expected as I drove north through the city, and after clearing the metro area, I was able to make up some time. I had called Cliff earlier to let him know I was back and would hopefully see him before sunset. At five after seven, I turned onto the property, and as the lake came into view, I saw a figure on the dock fishing. I parked, started down toward the dock, and as I got nearer, discovered it was new.

"How do you like it?" Cliff shouted as he slid his rod through the arm of his chair and stood up to give me a hug.

"It looks nice and expensive. I see someone took a little discretion with the budget."

"Michael, you have to admit the old dock was an accident waiting to happen with all those rotten boards and splinters. You didn't want little Nicole and Brittney around something like that."

"You're right. I just hope Mom likes it."

"She probably won't come."

"She'll see the invoice, Cliff."

"Yeah, I guess so, but I got a good deal. They didn't have to replace the pilings. Now that would have been expensive. They said the pilings were some sort of hardwood from Africa, and they would probably outlast the new decking."

"There is that."

"Hey, that crew was good. They finished the whole thing in three days. Tore down the old dock and replaced it with this."

"How did you find them?"

"Junior."

"That figures. For future reference, you might want to run something like this by me when you're giving me updates on a project."

"I thought it would be a nice surprise."

"It's okay this time, and like you said, the other one was a hazard. I think the kids will love it, and from what I can tell, it all looks great. I'm impressed."

"Thanks, Michael. I'm already packed, so I can be ready—"

I interrupted, "Cliff, why don't we stay tonight and leave tomorrow morning? I think I need the time, if that's okay."

"You bet."

"I'd get my rod, but it is a little late. Maybe we can fish a while before we leave tomorrow."

"That sounds like a winner, but we don't need to keep any more. I have already caught and cleaned enough for a meal or two, so I've been just releasing the ones I caught today."

"Okay."

"Have you eaten?"

"Just one of my energy bars a few hours ago."

"You and your bars. You're in for a treat, son. Let's go up to the house."

Forty minutes later, Cliff finished frying a mess of fresh-caught fish and hush puppies.

"You know, Michael, those cooking shows on TV always make a big deal saying fried chicken and mashed potatoes is the signature southern meal. In my book, this is right up there with it."

"I wouldn't disagree."

We ate as Cliff told me about his week. Then as we were finishing our meal, he asked me a question that pulled me back to Scotland and Caitie. I thought everything was going to be fine until that moment.

"Michael, did everything go as expected over there?"

I started to say something and then realized I didn't know how to explain it. It hurt too much, and the pain of leaving…how do you tell someone that? I knew I wouldn't make sense, so I stood up and started to walk outside.

"Michael, you need to talk to someone. I can tell you're upset, but unless you tell me what it's about, I am at a loss how to help you, son."

That was when I decided to tell someone I could trust the truth. "I want to be with her, Cliff. I don't care what the price is. I love her more than life, and honestly, I'm not sure I want to go on without her. I love Christy and the girls, but I had no idea what this would do to me, Cliff. The worst part is, I didn't tell her."

"What does Caitlin think?"

"Why the hell does that matter?" I snapped.

"Michael, it matters a great deal. And the fact that you are here and that question upsets you so much says a lot."

"Look, Cliff, it's just hard. I should have. I should have…"

"Michael, I'm flying blind here. Does Caitlin still have feelings for you?"

"She loves me, Cliff. Can you believe that? After all the crap my family did, she still loves me. They threatened her with rape, told her I no longer loved her, and her child does not know Caitlin is his mother. Cliff, she should hate me."

"Son, I told you Peggy plays hardball. Now what does Caitlin want you to do?"

"To go home. She wanted me to go back to the life I had before I read her letters. How can I, Cliff? She's sick, and she needs someone with her to give her the will to fight. She was crying when I left, and I'm such a damn coward I didn't tell her."

"Michael, she knows. I'm sure of that, and she has her family. They love her, and they will be there to give her the support she needs. What's the problem?"

"Brain tumor."

"That's bad. Does she at least get to see her son?"

"Yes, he's..." Then I recalled Caitie's wish. "Yes, she sees him, but like I said, he has no idea she is his mom."

"Michael, the important thing is, she gets to see him. Now I'm not saying you should forget Caitlin, but the fact that she felt it best for each of you to go back—"

"But I don't think she understood."

"Michael, I'm sure she knew how you felt. You may not have told her everything you said earlier, but—"

"Cliff, I'm not sure it would be fair to Christy and the kids."

"How fair would it be to leave them, Michael? I think Caitlin knew firsthand how—"

My phone rang, startling me. Cliff reached across the table and took the phone and walked away from me.

"Hello?"

"Michael, is this you?"

"No, Christy, this is Cliff. Michael went to town with Junior to get a belt for the truck."

"Okay."

"He left his phone, and I happened to hear it ring."

"So I guess you will be coming home tomorrow."

"Yes, that is our plan as long as they have the belt in stock."

"Fine, just have Michael call when he has a chance. The girls would like to talk to him."

"I'll be sure to tell him."

"Thanks, and bye."

Cliff laid the phone back on the table.

"I'll call her later, Cliff."

"Yeah. The girls wanted to talk to Daddy. You do know those girls are crazy about you."

"Yes, I know."

"Maybe that's why Caitlin thought it best to go back to the life you had before you found the letters."

"What do you mean?"

"Ryan is fourteen, and you missed all those years you could have been with him. Michael, if you were to leave your family to be with Caitlin now, you would miss many of those same years with Brittney and Nicole. I don't think Caitlin would want you to make such a sacrifice, and if you were being honest with yourself, you would realize it was the right thing to do."

"I do realize that, Cliff. It's just so unfair."

"Yeah, let me think about this. You have two women who are crazy about you. That's really unfair."

"You know what I mean."

"Yes, I do. It's just a shame you aren't a Mormon."

"Ha! Ha! Not funny. I don't believe either would approve."

"Well, how about a wrestling match…? Winner takes all."

"Like I said, not funny."

"Yeah, I guess I should have quit while I was ahead, but my money would be on Christy."

"She is competitive."

"That she is. Hey, I want you to take a look at a place Junior showed me the other day. I'm considering buying it, and it's only a few miles from here. You up to a little more riding?"

"Cliff, you do realize the sun has set?"

"We have lights, but I guess we could check it out on the way home tomorrow."

"I think that would be best. It seems you have found a real buddy in Junior."

"Hey, Junior is a keeper."

"From what I saw, I might have to agree."

"Now you're talking. Just give me a minute to clean up, and we can sit on the front porch and talk some more."

"Sure, I just need to go to the bathroom first."

"Okay, I'll see you outside."

As I washed my face with warm water, I realized Cliff had said nothing about my being so emotional. That was in stark contrast to Mom's philosophy. I also realized Cliff had let me vent without judgment. I think he knew just as Caitie and I both knew what had to be. I was going home to be with a family who loved me, and she was staying with those who loved her.

Chapter Twenty-Seven

I met Brittney and Nicole as they were walking into the garage.

"Daddy!" Brittney yelled as she saw me. I bent down to give her a hug.

"Miss me?" I managed as Nicole ran into my arms and made it a group hug. "This is what I missed so much, girls. You have to promise not to go away again."

Brittney looked at me with a puzzled expression then said, "Daddy, we didn't go away. You did."

"Oh, well. Thanks for coming back!"

Before Brittney had time to respond to what I said, Christy intervened. "Michael, you need to stop teasing them. They may develop a talent for it, like someone else we know."

"Okay, Mom, I promise to be good," I said as I released the girls after another hug. I stood and pulled Christy into my arms and kissed her. I sensed a tenseness and hoped it was the result of her being alone with the girls for the past week and not something else. "Everything okay?"

"Just tired."

"Okay." I started to say more but thought it best to say as little as possible for the present. Less said, less you have to walk back.

"Michael, Liz and Cal are meeting us at the park at five, and then we are going to dinner with them afterward. I hope you don't mind. Liz and I worked it out earlier."

"Sounds good. I forgot to tell the girls about the stuff, Cliff, and I got them. It's out in the truck."

"Let's give it to them later. We don't have long."

"Sure, I'll get it and put it in the pantry until we get back."

"That would be better." Christy then shouted up the stairs, "Girls, you need to change and potty! We have to leave in twenty minutes to meet the Masons at the park!"

"Okay, Mom!" the girls yelled in unison from upstairs.

Christy turned to me. "Well, how does it look? Did you get accomplished what you hoped to?"

"Yeah, it looks great. I think you and the kids will love it."

"Well, just so you know, you were missed."

"I know."

"Michael, I need to change into something more comfortable for the park and dinner," Christy said as she started up the stairs.

It was after nine before we got back home and put the girls in bed. I returned from tucking in the girls and walked over to Christy and kissed her. I sensed the tension again. "Everything okay?"

"No, it's not, Michael. Everything was good until Thursday, but since then, I have to admit my daughters have seen their mom drink a bit more than usual."

The worries I had concerning Christy picking up on the guilt I felt about Caitie vanished, but I realized I had not been listening to Christy when I noticed her staring at me.

"For the second time, I need a drink. Are you listening?"

"Yes, I mean no, but I am now."

"Well, you need to pay close attention because your brilliant wife royally screwed up while you were gone. Did you miss the part about the drink?"

"Coming up," I said as I walked over and chose a bottle of white wine—Christy's go-to for those moments when she had stepped in it. I turned to get a glass, and when I looked back, she was crying.

"Christy, it can't be that bad."

"Oh, it's bad."

I poured her a glass of wine. "Okay, take your time and tell me what happened."

"Are you going to listen?"

"Yes."

"That would be nice. A few minutes ago, you were in one of your damn fugue states. Well, while you were up in North Carolina playing in the dirt, I screwed up big time," Christy said as she finished her glass and pushed it over for another.

I could tell this was bad because whenever Christy would drink, she would always insist that those who were with her should also indulge. She was wired like that, and for something to cause her to go against her nature did not bode well. "I'm listening, Christy. Go ahead."

"Early in the week, there were some issues, but nothing bad. Just the usual. Nicole was sick for two days, and then Brittney got concerned you were not coming back. So I certainly hope it was worth it. I could not understand why you didn't just let Cliff and a couple of men go up there and clean the place up. The girls need you, Michael."

"I know, and I'll try to limit my business trips the next few months and give them some extra attention."

"That would be nice."

"Christy, let's get back to your story."

"Okay. I made it to Thursday. Think about that. Thursday! Then it went bad, and when I say bad, Michael, I mean bad. It all started that morning after I took the girls to day care. Your mom calls and proceeds to ask me if I had heard from you, and I said, 'Yes, I speak to him every day.' That's when your mom informed me she was concerned because she had not heard from you since you left. She then reminded me she was your mother and the CEO of the company you work for. Michael, I almost lost it. Where does that woman get off? But I calmly asked if she would like me to ask you to give her a call the next time we talked. She just said, 'No, it can wait' and hung up. Michael, I went nuts."

Christy passed her glass over to me again, and for a moment, I considered giving her a smaller pour but decided that would not be a wise move considering the mood she was in.

"That was just the beginning of my day of hell. Next, I went to my hair appointment with Raul, and he was out sick. So I rescheduled, then decided I would drop by Publix and pick up a few items. I was thinking at least I'll get something accomplished, and the day won't be a total waste. Well, I get home, and as I'm walking in, the bag with the two jars of spaghetti sauce rips open. The jars literally exploded when they hit the tile floor, and the sauce went everywhere. I thought about going back and giving them a piece of my mind. What moron can't figure it out? Double bag items of glass. If I had done so, I might have gotten it out of my system before I went to pick up the girls. But by the time I had put away the other items and cleaned up the mess, I didn't have time."

Christy pushed her glass over and motioned for me to keep it coming. This was concerning since Christy rarely went over three glasses of wine—her usual self-imposed limit. By my count, she was now sitting on five. She had two of the red at dinner and three of the white prior to the one I was now pouring. Those rare times when she exceeded this limit were when she was either very happy or very upset. I needed no superpowers to discern it was the latter.

Possibly sensing my reluctance to be party to her drowning her misery in a bottle, Christy reached across the island and took the glass then resumed.

"Anyway, like I said, after I cleaned up the mess, it was time to pick up the girls."

"That's a rough start, and you're saying it goes downhill from there?"

Christy slowly put her glass down and gave me this strange look. "Don't start that crap with me."

"Sorry, just trying to commiserate."

"So I get to the day care, and Ms. Tight-Ass herself asks if she could have a word with me. With the hellacious day I already had, the last thing I needed to endure was a conference with her. But no, no... Miss World Peace here says, 'Sure.'"

Christy pushed her glass back over. For a moment, I considered cutting her off, but once again, I thought it best not to push my luck. So I politely poured the remainder of the bottle into her glass. The Miss World Peace reference indicated to me this had entered uncharted territory, and I began to marvel at the composure Christy had shown at the playground and later at dinner with the Masons.

Christy loathed the nickname her brothers had given her, and in fact, I was certain this was the first time she had used it herself. The nickname was given to her due to what she often referred to as "not my finest moment."

To understand, you must know a little history. I was unaware of most of this prior to dating Christy, but due to the efforts of Christy and her mom, I was soon enlightened. Roseville was considered by many as a breeding ground for beauty queens. This was no understatement, and Christy became a part of this well-established program at an early age. In the over one-hundred-year history of the beauty pageant industry in Roseville, the area had produced sixteen Teen Misses, six Miss Georgia's, and one Miss America. The critical factor was, you must place in the top 2 in the Teen Miss competition, or the odds of successfully moving up to the next level was just short of winning the lottery.

In 1994, Christy was competing in the Teen Miss competition held annually in picturesque Columbus, Georgia. As a part of the competition, the contestants were all asked what they would choose as their signature issue if selected as that year's Teen Miss. Christy and her mother had been debating throughout the day as to which she would choose without deciding on a clear winner. So when the judges finally asked her which issue, Christy froze and said, "World Peace." Well, her brothers went nuts, and from that day forward, to the inner circle of brothers of the Walker family, she had been known as Miss World Peace. One of the judges later confided to Christy's mom that until that misstep, Christy had been in the top 2, so her moment had cost her the chance for her dream.

Christy had a rough life, growing up as this sweet, innocent girl with three elder brothers who were rough and very foulmouthed. I was shocked by her retort the first time I made a sarcastic remark in response to a question she asked me. Christy had asked if I thought anyone would notice the bump on her face, and without thinking, I replied, "No, I think it fits in nicely with the others." Christy fired back, "Shut the f——up!" I later learned this was her standard response to smart-ass comments made by her brothers. At the time, I think Christy could tell by the expression of disbelief on my face that it was not the response I expected. However, after hearing more about her childhood experiences with her brothers, I came to understand. Her brothers had confessed to me they would often tease her unmercifully until Christy would explode and unleash several choice expletives, which they had contributed to her vocabulary. A parent was invariably within earshot, so needless to say, she spent a fair amount of time in time-out or being the recipient of some other form of punishment. Christy often remarked, "How in the world those hellions turned out so well? I'll never understand."

The fact that she had such a tortuous day made me think she might have reacted before thinking, and if that were the case, I definitely needed to know. I noticed she was staring at me strangely again.

"Are you zoned out again? Hey, you need to listen, buster."

"Sorry, I may have been. Please continue."

"So the meeting with Webb starts out fine. We go into her office, and she starts with the usual yada yada crap. And I'm thinking, I got this. Then she says, 'Lately there have been concerns raised about Nicole's aggressive behavior during playtime.' Now I was familiar with at least one of those incidents she was referring to, and I was readying a defense on Nicole's behalf. I will confess, Michael, when Nicole told me the little Bradley boy bit her last week, I told her the next time he did that to hit the little shit as hard as she could."

Christy smiled at me as if she were waiting for me to congratulate her on her parenting skills. "Christy, tell me you didn't use those exact words, please?"

"What? You think she should take that? Hell no! No way. There were bite marks on her little arm. So as we are riding home Wednesday, she says, 'I hit him, Mom. Bing! Right on the nose.' Take that, you little shit."

I could tell the bottle had won the battle, and I wasn't sure Christy would make it to the point where I found out what happened. "Christy, I'm asking you if you used those exact words when you were talking to our three-year-old daughter." I was still under control, but I wasn't sure she heard me. So I repeated the question a little louder. I knew I was risking waking the two darlings upstairs and exposing them to a Mom/Dad moment, but I had to know.

"Hell no, I would never!" she blurted out as she stared at me like I was crazy for thinking such.

"Just checking, so you were at the point where Ms. Webb was talking to you about Nicole's aggressive behavior. Go ahead."

"I can't believe—"

"Sorry, please continue."

"Yeah. Then out of the blue, she says they are just concerned about how the issue might impact her behavior. Michael, I had no clue what the bitch was talking about, so I asked what issue. She looked at me in this strange way and repeated, 'The issue.' I look at her, and she is just staring at me like I was some dumbass. Now I must admit the thought did cross my mind that I may just have to hit this bitch, but I knew she was an older woman. So for the second time, I asked, 'What issue?'"

"That was very charitable of you, Christy."

"Shut the f——up, Mr. Smart-Ass."

"Please tell me there were no police involved."

"No. No police."

"Just concerned. This doesn't sound like it was going to end well."

"It didn't, but no police."

"Okay, try to finish. You need to get to bed."

"So then old Webb looks at me in this patronizing manner and starts wiggling in her chair with this strange expression on her face like I'm forcibly pulling it out of her. Then she says, 'Well, Ms. Williams, Nicole is obviously adopted.' Michael, I couldn't believe what she just said, so I asked, 'Why would you think Nicole's adopted?' Webb looks at me with this puzzled expression and says, 'Her eyes, Ms. Williams, her eyes. Remember, Michael went to this day care when I first opened it. He had the most beautiful blue eyes I'd ever seen, and yours are blue as well.' I lost it, Michael. I looked at that pompous bitch and said, 'I had a fucking affair. You got it? Michael has forgiven me, and if you repeat a word I've said, I'll come back down here and whip your butt.' Well, Webb just sat there frozen for a few seconds, and, Michael, I thought she had died. You know, had a stroke or something. Finally, I saw her eye twitch, so I just said that I think we are done here. Then she started nodding her head up and down like one of those bobbleheads, so I got the girls and left."

"I guess that explains what Brittney meant about them going to a new day care."

"Yes, and could you please go back there and apologize? I think I might die if I had to, and I don't want her talking, Michael."

"Okay."

"Please."

"Christy, are you listening? I said I would. Now we need to get you to bed."

"How will you explain that shit I said?"

"Well, I think we talked before I left about how you were supposed to make sure you took the meds your doctor prescribed for those times when you are stressed out."

"I screwed up, Michael. Poor Nicole. If there was one person that didn't know, they soon will and all because of me," Christy choked out as she burst into tears.

I went around the island and gently rubbed her back as she sat there weeping. I had to admit it was a mess. "Christy, I'll deal with it first thing tomorrow. I need to get you to bed."

"Do you think I'm drunk?"

I wisely let that go. It was too easy, and I worried she might start fighting.

"Hey. Hey. I'm talking to you. How the hell are you going to fix that?"

"Well, Christy, Ms. Webb did always think I was the golden child. She—"

"My ass. She was just kissing up to money. How does that help?"

"Let me finish. I was going to say you were going through a difficult time since the passing of your grandmother, and it was our hope that she could find it in her heart to forgive you for your bad behavior."

"Not sure that would work, Ace."

"Well, I was also going to suggest Williams Lumber donate the materials and labor to build a new playground for the day care. It has been past its prime for years."

Christy looked up and had this big smile on her face, and I knew I had her convinced I could pull it off. "Would you do that for me? Did I tell you that I love you, Michael?"

"Earlier."

Christy started crying again and pleaded, "Can you please carry me to bed, Michael? I don't think I can walk."

"Sure." Though I was not so sure. Christy had weighed only 115 pounds when we got married. She had the body of a ballerina. She had been groomed for competition with an exercise program and a strict diet that was closely monitored by the afore-mentioned brothers, who delighted in reporting her transgressions. Those often resulted in further disci-plinary action. It was a vicious cycle that her broth-ers reveled in as a means of further tormenting their sister.

Since our wedding, Christy had given birth to two children and had been free of any dietary regimen. So she ballooned to 130. Those were her words, not mine. Personally, I thought she looked better than the day we were married, but it didn't help that her mother would tell her she looked like she had put on weight almost every time she would see her. As I said, I think she looked better today, but weight is a factor when you are carrying someone up steep stairs.

Seeing no other option, I picked her up off the stool and started. I had made it about halfway up the stairs when she started tapping me on the shoulder, so I stopped. To be honest, I needed the break. "I'm sort of busy, Christy. Can it wait?"

"Hey, you better make it the biggest f——ing playground in the world, baby. I screwed up big-time."

I almost dropped her when she said that, but I just laughed and said, "I will" and started back up the stairs. I was now beginning to sweat, and I had a thought about what my mom used as her litmus test to decide whether I needed a bath or not as a child. She would always say, "Well, Michael, did you sweat? If you did, you need a bath." Christy and I had often violated that standard with the girls.

As I stepped on the landing, I felt a renewed surge of energy when I saw our bedroom. Victory was in sight. That was when she started tapping my shoulder again. "Michael, do you know why you are so lucky?"

Considering what we had been discussing the past hour, I was at a loss for what she meant. So as we were entering our bedroom, I asked, "What?"

"Why you are so lucky?"

"I don't understand."

"Because not every man gets to sleep with the second runner-up in the Teen Miss competition!"

When she said that, I lost it, started laughing, and tossed her onto the bed. She started crying again. That was when I made the mistake of getting too close to her. As I leaned over to apologize and console her, she took a wild swing and connected. After I assured her that I did indeed feel fortunate to sleep with the second runner-up in the Teen Miss competition, she smiled, turned over, and began to snore.

I went downstairs for a drink and some ice for my eye. As I sat there, I filed a comment to use if she brought up the fact that I should feel fortunate to sleep with the second runner-up at a future date. I would say I have to reserve comment until I see the two who placed above her. In her current state, she wouldn't have appreciated it. I also filed an additional mental note to make sure I was at least six feet away from Christy when I made that observation. Safety distancing!

The next morning, I told Christy to sleep in, and I would take the kids to day care.

"That eye looks rough, baby. What happened?" Christy managed as she rolled over to give me a kiss.

"Just clumsy. Go back to sleep," I said after I kissed her goodbye.

I dressed and fed the girls and then got Brittney to direct me to their new day care. Before I went to see Ms. Webb, I called ahead to arrange a meeting. After I assured her that I was not upset and only wanted to apologize, I noted a change in her tone. I could sense I still had my mojo.

Chapter Twenty-Eight

I walked into Mom's office at ten. She was reviewing the details concerning the acquisition of Clinch Lumber Company with her secretary, Jill.

"Michael, it's good to see you," she said as she smiled and walked over to give me a hug. "That eye looks bad. What happened?"

"Just caught a limb when I was helping clean out some brush."

"You might want to have it looked at."

"It'll be okay. It looks worse than it feels."

"Well, it's about time you got back to work. Jill and I were putting the finishing touches on the Clinch deal, but I still need you and Cliff to go there and take a look. We don't want any surprises."

"Tomorrow works for me. I need to catch up with a few things today, but I will get with Cliff later today and see if he is free to go tomorrow."

"Good. I hope your trip to North Carolina was worth it. We have been swamped, and I'm not so sure it wouldn't have been better to have waited on that particular project."

"Understood. Look, Mom, we need to talk when you are free."

"Let's talk now. Jill, make the changes we discussed, and I'll review it with you before lunch."

"Yes, ma'am," Jill said as she stood and walked out of the office, closing the door behind her.

"All right, what is this about, Michael?"

"I went to Scotland, Mom."

"What!" she shouted as she stood and glared at me. "Why the hell did you go there?"

"To apologize for the way our family treated Caitlin and to see my son. You know, the son you kept any knowledge of from me—that son!"

"My god, Michael! Does Christy know about this?"

"No."

"At least you haven't totally lost your mind. Michael, all that was handled. Your father even agreed it was best for the child to leave things as they were after he visited him in Scotland."

"And why didn't you go, Mom?"

Mom turned and looked out the large window that made up a good portion of the wall behind her desk. She just stood there, staring across the landscape covered by Williams Lumber. "I couldn't. I just couldn't."

I noticed a slight catch in her voice. "Maybe you were afraid to see what a wonderful child he was. It might have been harder to continue all the lies if you had held your grandson in your arms."

"No. No, it wasn't that. It was just that it was best—"

"Why didn't you let me read her letters, Mom?"

"Did she tell you about those?" Mom asked as she turned and stared at me.

"No, I found them in the attic when Becky and I were looking for the tree topper."

"I told Walter and Becky to burn those damn things. Why…? Why…?"

"And why did you send those fake letters to both of us?"

Mom glanced at me. "Isn't it obvious?"

"No."

"I thought it best for each of you to think the other had decided it had all been a mistake." Mom then looked at me as if she expected my approval then snapped, "I had to end it."

"It, Mom?"

"Michael, you need to let this go. It was a mess, and we handled it."

"Mess? You mean when Caitlin and I fell in love?"

"Love? My god, Michael, you were fifteen and had known this girl for only a week!"

"Strange, I didn't think there was an age or time requirement necessary for a person to fall in love.

In case you have forgotten, I think your aunt married when she was fourteen, and she seemed happily married the last time I checked."

"That was a different time."

"I don't understand how you could have suggested she have an abortion."

"It was just an option. I didn't force the issue."

"Even more troubling was discovering you had threatened to bring the charge of rape against Caitlin. Why would you do that?"

"Simple, Michael. It was."

"Trust me when I say this, Mom… It was not rape."

"Legally it was, Michael, and that was all that mattered. The age of consent in Georgia at the time was sixteen, and you were fifteen. Can't you see this was done to protect you, Michael?"

"Mom, you did it to preserve the Williams legacy."

"Why would you say that? But—"

"Simple. Because it's the truth."

"As I was going to say before you interrupted, yes, that was a part of the equation. Just not the most important part."

"What was the most important part, Mom?"

"Michael, can't you see it would have ruined your life? My god, you were entering your sophomore year of high school. Do you think you were actually ready for the kind of responsibility that comes with being a parent?"

"Maybe, if my family had been as supportive as Caitlin's was. Ryan seems to be a really good kid."

"That's right. He is doing good. I guess your father was right when he suggested we leave things as they were. You can't say how things might have been. Look at how things turned out."

"Mom, all I'm saying is, I should have been given a choice in the matter. I didn't meet Christy until I was twenty-three. If you or Dad had told me about Ryan in the interval, I would have had that choice. I don't see how you think you have the right to play God."

"For a good reason, Michael. We wanted you to have a normal life. Look at the family you have."

"Yes, Mom, but the point I am trying to make is, it would have been nice to know what was going on. It was my life. I should have been told. I was living a lie concocted with your fake letters and silence. Your actions denied me the chance at a life with Caitlin and Ryan."

"We didn't think it was worth the risk!"

"Risk?"

"Like I said, everything was working out. You were doing good in college. Ryan was doing great, and no one was the wiser. So why take the chance? You are making this sound worse than it was. We were concerned parents doing what we thought was best."

"Did you ever consider the effect of such deception on me or Caitlin? Let me tell you, it was tough on both of us. I couldn't understand how she could have suddenly changed, but then she didn't, did she, Mom?"

"I have no idea."

"Maybe we should talk to someone who may have suffered a similar fate."

"Who are you talking about?"

"Patsy."

"Leave her out of this. That was before your time, and you have no idea what you are talking about."

"I just wonder if Patsy would agree."

"The last I heard, she was happily married, with a bunch of grandkids. I don't think she's spent much time worrying about what she missed. Since you want to know the truth, Michael, Patsy did not share the same vision your dad had. She wanted to be Ms. Suzy Homemaker, and I believe she got her wish. Now what are your intentions? Michael, I hope you are not going to throw everything away for that damn woman."

"That damn woman? Mom, you have no idea what she is like. But to answer your question, no. Would you like to know why?"

"Why?"

"That woman you threatened and schemed against, that woman who still loves me—and by the way, I still love her too—told me I should stay with my family. How is that for a nefarious scheme, Mom?"

"Well, I'm glad one of you has some sense. Are we through? I do need to get some work done."

"One last thing."

"What?"

"I'm going to increase the amount of money we have been sending Caitlin to help with expenses. Ryan is planning to go to a university in a few years, and I should at least help with his education."

"Is this their request?"

"No, Mom. They did not ask for anything. I just thought, as his father, I should help financially since I may never be able to acknowledge Ryan as my son."

"If that is what you want."

"I'll see Tom and let him know so he can make the necessary arrangements."

"How did you know Tom handled the payments?"

"Just assumed." I could have said I was sure she did not want our name associated with payments being made to a young woman in Scotland but decided it might be best to let it go.

"Take care of it then."

"I definitely will, and I'll check with Cliff about going to the Homerville site tomorrow."

"Good, and, Michael, please don't think those were easy decisions. I pray you and Christy never have to face such decisions."

I was about to leave, but I realized I could not. She still had no idea of the harm she had done. "Mom, I don't think you fully understand the consequences of your deceit, especially concerning the letters you sent. Kathleen said Caitlin was at the brink of suicide after reading that letter, and it was weeks before she or Colin felt comfortable leaving her alone. That is hard for me to get past. You would have sacrificed Caitlin—the girl I loved—to preserve the Williams legacy. What you did was unconscionable. It's going to be some time before our relationship can return to normal. For now, I think it best to stick to business only."

"Michael, it wasn't easy making those decisions, and it impacted our lives as well. I'm sure the stress contributed to your dad's heart issues."

"Mom, don't go there. I'm sure living with you was a bigger factor than anything Caitlin and I did.

Having a relationship with Ryan may have actually been good for Dad's health, but you would not allow that. No, Mom, you might as well blame Becky while you're at it. I am sure seeing his daughter live with an abusive husband took its toll on Dad. It's called life, Mom."

"Michael, you know I… I love you."

"Yes, Mom, and I still love you. That's why it's so hard to understand how you could be so deceitful. We both need to get back to work before I say more."

"Okay."

I could tell she wanted to continue, but for some reason, she stopped. That was rare, and I was sure it was due to being surprised. I also knew she would be more formidable the next time I challenged her, and there would be a next time. "Mom, we will revisit this later. I need to get started."

"Yes, that might be best. Our focus needs to be on the Clinch deal for now."

"Understood," I said and turned to leave.

"Michael, could you ask Jill to come back in on your way out?"

"Sure."

And that was it. As I walked out of Mom's office, I knew this was the first confrontation with her in which I had come out as the possible victor. Even more telling was how much she revealed, and I was sure when she mulled over our argument, she would realize it. Maybe Cliff was right; I did have some of Mom in me. God help me.

Chapter Twenty-Nine

The rest of my morning had gone surprisingly well. I briefly met with Cliff and then rode out to check on a few of the sites nearby, where crews were harvesting profit, as Cliff put it. When I returned, I went through the lumberyard and store, talking with a few of the employees to assess how things were going. As I was doing this, it came to me that I needed to try to do what Dad was so good at—building a loyal team. I knew a big part of doing that was what I had done today. I had some ideas of my own, and I knew, when I reassumed the leadership of Williams Lumber in a few years, it would not be a repeat of my first experience. Foremost of those ideas was the rebranding of Williams Lumber as Twin Oaks Lumber. That had been a recurring thought of mine over the past few months, and I was waiting for the right time to pitch the idea to Mom. Needless to say, it was not going to be today. I was reviewing those ideas and weighing the merits of each with the intention of preparing a document that outlined my vision for the future of the company. I knew if the company was going to continue to grow, there were areas that needed to be addressed, and in my opinion, none was more important than employee satisfaction. We had to give them a reason for wanting to continue to be a part of our company.

I made it back to my office at one thirty. As I walked in, I saw Becky sitting at my desk. She had her back to me and was looking out the window down onto the lumberyard. When I closed the door, she swiveled the chair around to face me and smiled.

"Great view."

"Yes, I find it mesmerizing at times. It's like an ant farm." I was puzzled. This was not like Becky, and my first thought was, *Something must be wrong.* I could see a look of concern on her face. "Is everything okay, sis?"

"Mom called after the two of you had your talk this morning."

I didn't know how much Becky knew about Mom's actions concerning Caitie. "I thought it was time someone let Mom know the impact it has on people when she plays god."

"I thought they should have said something to you when you graduated from college, Michael."

"It would have been nice. Does your husband know?"

"No, Mom and Dad thought it was best to keep it in the immediate family for obvious reasons."

"Obvious reasons?"

"Michael, my first marriage didn't work out so well."

"Did you know they threatened Caitlin?"

"I know some of what went on, Michael, but I'm sure there was more. Mom is Mom."

"Becky, they were going to charge her with rape."

"Michael, it never came to that."

"Only because Mom got what she wanted."

"I'm not sure what I would have done in a similar situation. They were worried it might ruin your life."

"So they chose to possibly ruin Caitlin's instead."

"Is she okay?"

"It's complicated."

"What do you mean?"

"She's doing okay career-wise, I suppose. She is a junior officer in a bank in Edinburgh, but she is sick, Becky." I didn't know how much she knew about Ryan, so I felt it best to say nothing about him. It was not that I didn't trust Becky. It was more a case of respecting Caitie's wishes. The less who knew, the better.

"Sick? How bad is it?"

"Bad. She has a brain tumor."

"Oh my, will she have surgery?"

"Her doctor has scheduled a biopsy, and she is seeing a specialist this week. But no decision has been made yet concerning her treatment. I just assume it will involve radiation or surgery or possibly both."

"If it's benign, wouldn't they leave it alone?"

"She's having these fainting episodes."

"How often?"

"I know she has had two over the past few weeks."

"That has to be scary."

"The tough thing is, she doesn't want me to call, Becky. So I have to wait until her mom or dad contact me."

"I'm sure that is hard, Michael. You still have feelings for her, don't you?"

I looked at my sister and, for a moment, thought about how I should answer that question. "More than you would approve of Becky."

"And does she feel the same?"

"Yes."

"But, Michael, you have such a sweet wife."

"Yes, Becky, and I love her. But it doesn't change the way I feel about Caitlin."

"Oh, Michael, that has to be so difficult."

"I have my moments."

"I'm sure. But there is something I must tell you, and I hope you won't hate me for what I did."

"Becky, what are you talking about?"

"The letter. The letter you thought was from Caitlin. The letter in which Caitlin told you she thought it was best if you both went back to the life before the two of you met."

"Yes, Becky, I'm aware of the letter. It was a fake."

"Well, I wrote it."

"What? Why would you do that?" But I knew the answer before she said the words. I stared at Becky as she fought to hold back the tears. I had been so in love with her as a child, yet twice, she had been a factor in destroying any hope I might have had of a life with Caitie. The first had been by chance. This was intentional and was a betrayal of that love.

"Mom thought the only way to save you was if you believed Caitlin felt it had been all a mistake."

"Well, you certainly worked your magic, sis. Thanks."

"I deserve that, and I'll understand if you can't forgive me. I just knew I needed to tell you and apologize for my part in the deception. I am truly sorry, Michael."

"What about the letter that was sent to Caitlin?"

"Michael, I only wrote the one letter to you. Mom gave me Caitlin's letters so I would get the feel for how she wrote, and then I wrote the one letter. If it helps, I'm not proud of what I did."

I just stood there thinking maybe I should tell her how much Caitie suffered. Maybe then she would start to realize the damage she had been party to when she chose to write that letter, but I decided to say nothing. What would it change?

"Michael, I'm ashamed and truly sorry for the part I played in deceiving you, but I have to leave to pick up Eli in a few minutes."

"Sure."

Becky came around the desk and hugged me. "I do love you, Michael, and I'm sorry to hear about what Caitlin's going through. Please let me know how she is doing when you find out."

"Okay. Love you too, sis," I said reflexively, and that was it. I then watched her walk out and close the door. I sensed Becky had some idea of the pain her actions had caused, but as I continued to stare at the door, the only thought I had was, *I'm not sure I can ever forgive any of you for what you did.*

It's the circle of life.

As one leaves this world,

another enters.

—CC

PART 2

Omega and Alpha

Chapter Thirty

Roseville, 2019

I always thought I would learn that Caitie was near death with a late-night call. Then I would rush to her side just before she died to reaffirm my love. That wasn't how it happened.

It was a Thursday in August, and it had been a good morning until my secretary brought in the mail. I started to flip through it, and there it was—a small plain envelope with a return address of Edinburgh, Scotland. I hesitated since I rationalized there would be plenty of time. There was no rush, or surely someone would have called. But why was there no name on the return address?

Fifteen years. It was hard to believe so many years had passed since I last saw Caitie. Though I still loved her, my love for Caitie had evolved as had my love for Christy. I continued to write Caitie a letter once a year for her birthday since I last saw her sitting on the couch, smiling at me. My hope was she would be able to see my life through my words, and thus would share it with me. I did my best. Though on occasion, I would mention something only she and I would understand. My hope was this would let her know she still held a special place in my heart.

I knew some would say I was being unfair to Christy. However, if a person asked Christy about our life together, she would have said some people are fortunate enough to meet and marry the love of their life, and she had been one of those people. My answer to that same question would have been different. I would have said Christy had shown me there were second opportunities in the search for one's true love. Unfortunately for me, I found out several years too late that I was not in need of such an opportunity.

I began to open the letter then stopped. I picked up my jacket, slipped the letter into my pocket, and walked out of my office. I thought it unlikely that I would be in the mood to meet with anyone after reading the letter. I stopped at my secretary's desk. Cathy was filing some documents, and I waited until she turned and noticed me.

"I didn't know you were there, sir. Do you need anything?"

"Yes, I need you to move my afternoon appointments to later in the week. I'm leaving, and I may not be back today."

"Yes, sir. It shouldn't be a problem. There were only two, and I'll call them now."

"I appreciate it, Cathy. Something came up that I need to take care of today. If I don't make it back in, I'll see you tomorrow."

"Yes, sir."

That was the good thing about being the boss. Employees don't usually question your actions, and they are often eager to please. It also helped that most of the employees were under the delusion that I could do no wrong. Cliff often joked that some of the more recent additions to our team thought I was some sort of superhero. Most of the employees had been with our company for less than fifteen years. The past eight since I reassumed the role as CEO had been the best years the company had ever experienced, and they had benefited substantially.

As I walked through the office and out through the showroom floor, each employee I passed seemed compelled to say something to me. I acknowledged each with a nod or a brief reply when necessary, but if there was such a thing as an invisibility cloak, I would definitely run it by purchasing. As I continued out the door and started for the parking lot, I met Cliff.

"Michael, are we still on for lunch today?"

"Sorry, Cliff, something came up that can't wait."

"Okay?"

I could tell he was puzzled and I knew Cliff had stopped as I walked past him, but the fact I hadn't stopped spoke to the urgency of what I was doing.

It was a priority, and I didn't have time to chat. I turned slightly and threw, "We'll talk later, Cliff" as I continued walking toward my truck.

At first, I just drove, and then I knew where I needed to be when I opened the letter. Actually, I had to settle for my second choice. My first choice was where I first kissed Caitie, but I thought my mom might think it was a little strange if I walked in and asked to use Becky's old bedroom for a few minutes. So I drove to Twin Oaks, and thankfully Mom was gone. I parked and walked around to the back of the house. Thirty years ago, I had demonstrated my carving skills to Caitie on one of the several magnolias that Mom and Dad planted when they did the landscaping for the area around the house. I carved our initials inside a heart, and she had kissed me.

The sun was directly overhead, and though it had been in July instead of August, it felt like a similar day. I held the letter as I stared at the return address just to be certain it was what I read earlier.

I finally decided it was time, so I carefully opened the envelope and pulled out the folded note that was inside. It read:

Michael.
Please call,
011-44-131-556-5898.

I stared at the note for a moment, then took out my smartphone, and called the number. A few seconds later, I heard a voice.

"I need to take this."

I suddenly realized it was around 4:00 p.m. in Edinburgh and thought it might have been better to have waited a few hours to make the call, but it was too late. The voice came back on the line.

"Hello," the voice said.

"Hello, this is Michael Williams, and I just received a card with instructions to call this number."

"Yes, Michael, this is Kathleen, Caitlin's mum. She asked me to call to let you know…" Then her voice faltered, and I could tell she was emotional.

"Is she okay?"

"No, Michael, we lost Caitlin. It was a week ago, and I'm still having my moments."

I couldn't speak. I was numb, even though it was what I feared. For a moment, my body had lost its ability to function as I tried to process what to say. Finally, I heard Kathleen's voice again.

"I know this is a shock, Michael, but it was what she wanted. She also told me to give you something. There is no rush. If you prefer, I could mail it to you to keep from having to make the trip to Scotland."

"No." I had finally regained the ability to speak, but I was unsure if what I had just said made sense.

"I'm not sure I understand."

"I'm sorry. I will come to Scotland as soon as I can arrange it. It may be a few weeks, and I apologize…"

"There's no hurry, Michael. That's fine."

"May I call this number when I have made my plans?"

"Yes. It will be great to see you again. I hate to cut this short, but I need to go. So just call me when you have made your plans."

"I will."

"Bye."

The phone went dead, and that was how I learned I had lost a woman I would always love. I had cried three times in my life, and by that, I mean really cried. I teared up often, such as when I watched a sad movie with Christy or the kids, when my kids did something special, or when I heard a song or read something that touched me or rekindled a special memory. Those times were when my father died, when I realized I most likely would never see Caitie again, and when my daughter tried to commit suicide.

Nicole was having a rough time when she turned thirteen, and then she found out she was not my biological daughter. It had been too much, and she had tried to overdose on some of her mother's meds. Fortunately, she threw up most of the pills, and the rest were pumped out of her at the ER. That had been our warning. We were given a second chance, and we were determined to take full advantage of it. Nicole, Christy, and I went to counseling sessions. We even contacted Phil Parrish, her biological father, and arranged for her to have sessions with just the two of them and a psychologist. Phil assured Nicole that he loved her, but he felt it was logical for her to stay with her mom.

Nicole even started staying overnight with Phil when he came down from Atlanta to visit his mother. Phil had worked as a lawyer in Roseville but, after the affair, felt it best if he moved. His reputation made the transition easy, and he was currently working with a large firm in Atlanta. After several visits with Phil, Nicole decided she might consider a career in law. Her mother and I were just happy that we had seen a lot more smiles on her face lately, that her grades were up, and that she had made some friends who seemed good for her. Her mom and I were also glad we had finally reached a point where the topic of our conversation when we were alone was something other than whether Nicole was going to be okay.

This was the fourth time. I was so upset I had not noticed Mom had returned home and was standing behind me.

"Michael, is it one of the kids?"

I turned and saw a look on her face I had rarely seen. She looked genuinely concerned. Without thinking, I blurted it out, "She's gone, Mom. Caitlin's gone."

Then she did something that made me think she might actually have a heart. She pulled me into her arms, hugged me, and said, "It's always so hard when you lose one you truly love, Michael." She continued to hold me as I cried and, after a minute or so, patted me on my neck and suggested we go inside for a drink.

Since retiring three years earlier at the age of seventy-two, Mom had put her energy into two passions—spending time with her six grandkids and one great-grandkid, and cooking. The exposure to children who loved her unequivocally might have been a factor in the development of the aforementioned heart. I, on the other hand, lived through her era of tyranny, which was impossible to forget and hard to forgive. Scars had a way of serving as reminders, even though they were emotional.

Mom had honed her cooking skills by preparing two or three meals daily. On the off chance you drop by, you will be offered an opportunity to sample her latest culinary fare. She donated most of her cooking efforts to a local homeless shelter that had Twin Oaks Lumber as one of its sponsors, and I had heard many of the regulars at the shelter rave about her offerings. I suppose caring for your fellow man might help further explain the emergence of said heart. If I were being honest, I would have to admit she was always a good cook.

We talked as I tried to eat a small portion of a chicken and rice casserole.

"Do you know what happened, Michael?"

"No, Mom. Kathleen just told me Caitlin had died and that she had left me something she wanted me to have."

"Are you planning to go to Scotland?"

I was thinking about how I was going to manage that, and I had no idea. I knew when my brain started fully functioning again, I would work it out. I had to go. It was the least I could do for Caitie. She had always been the one who had to sacrifice.

"Michael, are you listening?" Mom shouted.

"What?"

"Going, Michael. Are you going? It's a simple question."

Mom had lost none of her ability to stay on topic. She was determined to find out my intentions. "What do you think?"

"You're a lot like your dad, so you'll go."

"Why do you say it like you think it's the wrong thing to do?"

"Because I feel it is, Michael, but that's just my opinion."

"Mom, I'll simply fly over, see the family, get whatever it is Caitlin wanted me to have, and come back home. I don't see the harm in that."

"Maybe you should ask your wife what she thinks about that idea, Michael."

I pushed my unfinished plate away. It was no use. Mom had crossed into territory she had no right to be in.

"Michael, whatever you decide will be fine, and you know this conversation stays between us."

"Thanks for the meal, Mom." Noting she had brought out the infamous code of silence that was a trademark of her reign at Williams Lumber, I made a mental note to reassess those earlier thoughts I had concerning her heart.

"Caitlin has always been a sensitive subject, Michael."

"Don't worry yourself, Mom."

"Michael, a parent always worries about matters that impact their children. I think you should know that by now."

"Okay, Mom, but I gotta go." I had reached my level of tolerance for Mom and knew it was best to leave. I then went over to Mom, gave her a hug, and walked out to my truck.

As I drove between the two oaks, I pulled into the shade of one of the massive trees. "Why! Why didn't you call me, Caitie!" I shouted as I stared at the tree.

Chapter Thirty-One

As far as my family and other interested parties knew, I was finalizing a deal to purchase several properties in the Orlando area. Tom and I would go down early Friday morning, do a final tour of the properties, and then if all parties were satisfied, complete the purchase. The realty company had asked me to look at some additional properties on Saturday that were being developed. This would take most of the day, so Tom and I would drive back early Sunday morning.

The initial part of the plan was simple. I knew the group in Orlando would work with me since they had clients who were eager to sell. The difficult part was finding a date that made it possible for me to make the trip to Edinburgh and return in the time frame of about thirty-six hours. Fortunately, a lot of people visit Disney World, and so there was a 1:00 a.m. flight that few directly to London with a connecting flight to Edinburgh at 7:00 a.m. on Saturday. That would give me about ten hours in Edinburgh since my return flight was at 7:00 p.m. on Saturday with a connecting flight out of London at 9:15 p.m. However, I would be flying back to Atlanta since there were no flights to Orlando at a time that worked. It was tight but doable. I would just get a rental and meet Tom in Roseville on Sunday morning.

When all was set, I called Kathleen's number. It was almost 8:00 p.m. in Scotland, and the call was accepted after the first ring.

"Hello."

"Hello, is this Kathleen?"

"Yes."

"This is Michael Williams. I called to let you know I have made arrangements to come to

Edinburgh in eight days. I will arrive early Saturday morning. I just wanted to make sure that it was a convenient time for you."

"Yes, that will work out nicely. It will be good to see you, Michael."

"It will be good to see you as well. I should be at the hotel a little before nine, and I'll call you after I check in."

"That's fine. We are usually up by six, so any time after that is good. Michael, I am so glad you are able to come. I just wish it were under different circumstances."

"Me too. Well, I guess I'll see you then."

"Bye, Michael. We'll talk then."

"Okay. Bye."

The next seven days were a mix of anxiety and fear for me—anxiety at the prospect of reentering Caitie's family without her being there and fear that any number of things might go wrong that would necessitate a change in my plans. It was not easy as I waited for the days to slowly pass.

Friday finally came, and I rode down to Orlando with Tom early that morning. Our accountant, Gary, was driving down later in the day. He was actually much more than just an accountant. He had become a trusted financial adviser over the past five years, and together we were moving Twin Oaks Lumber in a new direction. Seven years ago, he had suggested there were sounder uses of cash on hand than merely investing it in stocks and bonds. After a year, I was convinced, and since that time, we had acquired two car dealerships and made several real-estate purchases for rental purposes. Initially, I was concerned about what Dad would have thought, but Mom had assured me he would have been proud. When she said, "You are moving the company into the future," I knew it was the right thing to do.

I met briefly with the representatives of the realty company and their lawyers. I informed them they could reach me by phone and that Tom was to serve as my legal proxy in all the negotiations. After thanking them for being so cooperative, I took a taxi to the airport and, ten hours later, landed in

London. Thankfully, I was able to sleep a few hours on the flight.

I got a room at one of the hotels in Heathrow. Though it would only be for a few hours, I was certain it was worth the price. I could relax without worrying about missing my connecting flight, so I asked them to give me a call at five thirty since the flight to Edinburgh departed at seven.

As I lay on the bed, I thought about how different my life would have been if Caitie and I had been given a choice. I was no longer angry about her not calling me, but it was hard to face the reality that she was gone. The last thing I remembered was staring at a clock that read three thirty and thinking how much I missed Caitie.

Chapter Thirty-Two

The plane landed in Edinburgh at eight thirty, and I was checking into my hotel at nine. It was a tight schedule, but I reminded myself that I was about to meet Caitie's parents, and they had just lost a daughter who meant the world to them. The fact that Christy and I had almost suffered a similar fate made it easy to understand what they were experiencing, but they deserved so much more than I could give them. I knew I had to do this right.

I couldn't stay in the same hotel. It had too many memories, so I got a room in a hotel that was closer to her parents' home and the airport as well. The driver recommended a Marriott, which I called en route. Fortunately, they had a room available. It was only to serve as a place to drop my bag and freshen up since I would be flying home at 7:00 p.m. that day.

After checking in, I called Kathleen. She answered on the second ring.

"Hello."

"Is this Kathleen?"

"Yes."

"Good morning. This is Michael. I just wanted to be sure it was okay to come over in a few minutes."

"Yes, and I hope you haven't eaten because I'll have a hearty Scottish breakfast of tattie scones, eggs, sausage, and coffee ready."

"That sounds delicious, but you don't have to do that for me. I usually carry something to get by on."

"It's no problem, Michael."

"Okay, I'll see you in a few minutes then."

"We'll be here."

That was when my nerves kicked in, so I went to the bathroom and took a look in the mirror.

This habit hearkened back to my mom's insistence that a member of the family should present a certain image. As I stared into the mirror, my assessment was that I was above the threshold Mom demanded—presentable.

Twenty-five minutes later, I was walking up to the house where I last saw Caitie fifteen years earlier. I held my breath, knocked, and waited. A few moments later, the door opened.

"Come in. Come in, Michael," Colin said. As I stepped in, he embraced me. "It's good to see you, lad."

"It's good to see you too, sir. I was sorry to hear about Caitlin."

"Thanks. It has been difficult for us all."

I followed as Colin led the way. As I entered the kitchen, Kathleen smiled, walked around the table, and hugged me.

"Caitlin would be so happy you came, Michael."

"Thank you. I appreciate that you let me know," I said as I struggled for the right words. I wanted to ask why they had denied me the chance to see her before she died, but I knew I had long ago lost any right to say something like that to Kathleen.

"I'm going to go to the pub and help Ryan get ready to open up," Colin said as he took his coat off a chair. "I guess I will be seeing you later, Michael."

"Yes, sir," I said as he started to walk away. I struggled to think of what I should say then decided it was better to say nothing. Less is more. I then turned my attention to Kathleen, who was motioning for me to take a seat.

"Breakfast is ready," Kathleen said as she set two platters on the table in front of me. One had sausages and eggs, and the other, scones. "The coffee should be cool enough to drink," she added as she poured me a cup.

I sat down, added two teaspoons of sugar to the coffee, stirred it, and took a sip. "Good."

"Thank you."

"This looks delicious," I said as I took a scone and then used my fork to put an egg and two sausages on my plate.

Kathleen smiled. "Colin is going to pick you up at one and take you to the cemetery."

I could tell it affected Kathleen when she said that last word, but I was glad to hear that I would be seeing Colin again. "I appreciate that. I'm sure it has not been easy."

"No, it hasn't, Michael," Kathleen said as she wiped the tears from her eyes.

I took a sip of coffee and set the cup down. "I feel like I need to apologize to your family again."

"Michael, you sound like Colin. A few years ago, we were sitting in our garden, and he says, 'I sometimes wish I had made that trip to see Walter by myself.' After I pointed out to him that there would have been no Ryan if Caitlin had not gone with him, he just sat there for the longest time, staring at the flowers. Then he said, 'I'm sorry I said that. Ryan makes every day of my life special.' Ever since that day, Colin has had a different attitude about what happened. So, Michael, there's no need to apologize."

"Kathleen, I hope you and Colin realize how much your daughter meant to me."

"We know, Michael."

I thought I'd waited long enough. I had to know what happened, so I asked, "Kathleen, was it a tumor?"

Kathleen took a sip of coffee and sat there in silence. For a moment, I thought she must not have heard what I said, but then she spoke. "Yes, the doctor said the scan showed a tumor, and he feared it was malignant. After further tests, he told us nothing could be done. He apologized to Colin and me and said that there are times when it is best not to fight because it would only cause more pain and suffering, and he felt this was one of those times. Michael, she didn't suffer. She was so—"

I could see the tears in Kathleen's eyes. "I'm sorry. I just had to know."

"I understand, Michael," Kathleen said as she took a tissue from her pocket and wiped the tears before she continued. "She went to all the follow-ups. It just moved too fast. There was nothing that could be done." She wiped her tears again with the tissue and just sat there in silence for a moment.

"I know it has to be hard to talk about, but it is comforting to know that she didn't suffer."

"Yes, we were thankful for that."

I had learned what I needed to, so I decided to move the conversation to something less distressful for Kathleen. "Did I hear Colin say he was working with Ryan?"

"Yes, Ryan has been working at the pub the past few months. He and Sophie want to buy a house, and working there on the weekends would give him the opportunity to earn some extra money for the down payment."

"That sounds good. I guess Sophie is his girlfriend or wife?"

"Wife. They have been married for two years now. She is so sweet, and Caitlin was quite fond of her."

"That's wonderful."

"The funny thing is that Ryan has enjoyed working at the pub so much he is considering going into the business with Colin."

"Will he make as much working at the pub?"

"Actually more."

"That is good."

"Yes, across the pond, you have a different pay scale for engineers. He'll make a good deal more at the pub once he starts full-time."

"A win-win, as people say."

"How so?"

"He will be doing something he enjoys and will also make more money."

"I see."

"Kathleen, when I first called, you mentioned Caitlin had left something for me."

"Yes, and I believe it is time for you to see what it is. There is a young lady waiting in our garden with Caitlin's gift."

"Okay, and who is the young lady?"

"It's a surprise, Michael, and I imagine she is probably concerned by now that I have forgotten to send you out back. I think it may be best if you go see her, and we will talk some more a little later."

"Okay," I said as I tried to think of who it could be. My first thought was Erin. But Kathleen had said "young lady," and that was not the way I would have described Erin since she had to be in her late thirties or early forties. Remembering my last encounter with Erin, I made a mental note not to say anything about the young lady not being an accurate description, if it were her. Then I settled on Sophie. She was the right age, and the way Kathleen acted when she mentioned her name told me she was loved by the family. She also married our son, so it was only natural for her and Caitlin to have been close the past few years.

"I think I may know who it is."

"Let's not spoil Caitlin's surprise, Michael."

"Yes," I said, and then I stood, walked around the table to Kathleen, and gave her a hug.

"I'm sorry I wasn't here. I loved Caitlin so—"

"I know, Michael. It was what she wanted."

I didn't understand, but as I said, I had no right to question any decision Caitie or her family made. I then turned and walked over to the door, I assumed, went to the garden. I looked back at Kathleen, and she nodded, confirming my assumption.

Chapter Thirty-Three

I was amazed when I opened the door and stepped out into the garden. It was unexpected and so wondrous. There was a path that seemed to encircle a central area of floral imaginings, and it separated the bed from the colorful shrub-like plants that served as a border for the Campbell's property. The path was paved with irregular-shaped stones, and I could imagine small children making up games that involved skipping across the stones.

I looked both ways and decided to go left. The dazzling display of flowers was surprising and reminded me of a garden I might see in Roseville.

Though I had never claimed to be a student of horticulture, I did recognize several varieties of rhododendrons.

I continued down the stone pathway and soon arrived at the top of what I now realized was an oval-shaped path. There I found a young girl, sitting on a bench, looking at what appeared to be a large notebook. I was puzzled. She's too young. This can't be Sophie. She must have heard my approach because she closed the notebook, looked at me, and smiled.

"Hi, I'm Chloe, your daughter."

I was stunned. What had the girl said? The young girl sitting on the bench had said something I was sure I had misunderstood. How could...

"Mr. Williams, I'll make room. Please sit with me on the bench," Chloe said as she slid to one side of the bench. "Or if you prefer, you can sit in one of the chairs."

"That might be best," I managed. My mouth was suddenly dry as I struggled to think of what to say. "Your mom, she never said..." And then my brain temporarily stopped functioning as I took a close look at this beautiful young girl, who had just informed me she was my daughter. She had auburn hair, green eyes, and delicate long fingers, and she was several inches taller than her mom. She was only fourteen, a year older than my son James. I could hear Caitie laughing at me as I struggled to understand how this could be.

I realized I had been staring at Chloe for quite some time without saying anything, so I took a seat in one of the chairs near the bench. The chairs and bench were positioned so each had a good view of the central bed and made for easy conversation among those sitting there, admiring the view. I could imagine the family sitting there, looking over the beautiful flowers at the end of the day, enjoying themselves. As I tried to think of what to say, Chloe spoke.

"I suppose you were trying to say Mum never said anything about me to you."

"Yes, that," I managed.

"She told me a few years ago she thought it was best not to say anything to you."

Listening to Chloe, I suddenly realized how uncaring I must seem. This beautiful young girl had recently lost the only parent she knew, her mother, who loved her dearly. Yet I, her father, had said nothing to try to comfort her.

"She always told me not to worry. Mum said she and her family would make up for any shortcomings caused by the absence of my father." Chloe paused as a single tear slowly moved down her cheek, and for a moment, she glanced down at her hands before looking up at me and continued, "But she's gone now, and I miss her terribly."

I looked at Chloe, and I felt the pain all parents who love their children feel when their child is suffering and they are unsure what they can do to ease the pain.

Then Chloe looked at me, and what I heard was Caitie's voice, "Could you please hold me?"

As tears streamed down the face asking me to prove my love, I moved over to the bench and took her in my arms. "I am so sorry, Chloe. I wish I had known how seriously ill your mom was. I would have come. I loved her so. If I had just known, I would have found a way to see you both. Please forgive me. I will find a way to make you a part of my life. I will make you that promise, Chloe."

Chloe pulled away from me. "Mum said she didn't want to do anything to harm your family, Mr. Williams. I have my grandparents, Ryan, Sophie, and my friends. I will be fine. It's just—"

"Chloe, I understand. I lost my father, but I was much older. I can't imagine what it would have been like if I had been your age and lost the only parent I knew."

Chloe wiped her tears with a tissue. "I have a present for you from Mum and me. But first, is it okay if I call you Dad?"

"I'm not sure I deserve to be called that, Chloe." What I wanted to say was, How could you ever consider me as your dad?

"Why would you say that?"

"Chloe, you don't know anything about me, and—"

Chloe interrupted, "Yes, I do. I love you, Dad."

I turned away so she would not see how much those words had affected me. How could this beautiful angel love me? I wiped my eyes. She had no idea who I was, and she should hate me. I chose to live a life with another woman instead of her mother. How could I explain that to Chloe? I knew I couldn't. "Chloe, how…how could you possibly know about me?"

"The letters and Mum."

"The letters?"

"Yes, Mum let me read the letters you wrote to her each year and the ones you wrote to her when you came to Scotland fifteen years ago."

"She let you read those also?" I asked as I tried to recall what I had written.

"Well, she did make a copy of one that had a small portion of it marked out."

"Okay." Though I couldn't remember exactly what I had written that needed to be censored, I was sure it concerned Ryan.

"When I was little, she told me it was some bad words, but a few years ago, she told me she would tell me what it concerned if I stopped asking questions about it. I agreed. Then she told me it was about a member of the family, and it would hurt them very badly if they were to ever learn what it said."

"Sounds bad."

"I thought it was probably something you said about my grandparents. I have noticed some of the things Uncle Ryan says about his in-laws are not that nice. They don't seem to have a good relationship."

"It happens, but I don't see how the letters could—"

"I said letters and Mum. I should have said Mum and letters. I was always inquisitive about you, and she would answer my questions. She also showed me the photos."

"Photos?"

"Yes, the photos she took when she went to Roseville."

"Oh my, I completely forgot she did have a camera."

"Yes, and she took forty-eight pictures, which she put in an album. So I got her to enlarge one, and I have it in my room beside a photo I have of her."

"I guess I looked a little young?"

"When you are five, those things don't really matter."

"I guess not. Is that what's in the notebook?"

"No, the album is at home. Mum wanted you to know what our life was like, so we each made a notebook for you." Chloe then took the large notebook and handed it to me. "This is Mum's. It has the letters you wrote her each year along with the ones Mum wrote in response to yours."

I started to ask Chloe if she was aware that her mom had never sent any of those letters to me but decided it was best not to raise the point at the time. I flipped open the cover and saw a picture I had forgotten about. It was taken the afternoon we explored Old Town together. We were in a small bar we had gone to after our late lunch. We were holding each other, and it gave the appearance we were a young couple in love, enjoying life.

"And this is mine. Though technically, mine and Mum's. It has a picture of me on each of my birthdays, and starting at the age of three, I wrote or drew something for you. We also chose some pictures or other items to include concerning things I did during the year."

"I'm at a loss for words. Thank you, Chloe. I can't express how much your thoughtfulness and understanding mean to me."

"Mum didn't give me any choice in the matter."

"How so?"

"If I ever said anything about you not loving us enough to be with us, she would defend you. She often said that one day you would come to see me and then I would see for myself the kind of person you are."

I couldn't speak, and then I heard a voice shout. "Chloe, it's time!"

"I'm coming," Chloe answered, and then she looked back at me and continued, "It's my piano lessons. On Saturdays, I take private lessons at university from eleven to twelve. I must go, but I hope to see you later." We both stood, and Chloe gave me a hug, kissed me on the cheek, and said, "Love you, Dad."

"I love you too, Chloe," I surprisingly responded. I then sat down and watched as Chloe walked back toward the house, and in a moment, she was gone. I just stared at the flowers as I tried to make sense of all that had transpired. My thoughts were interrupted by the sound of approaching footsteps, and as I looked up, I saw Kathleen come into view. She had a big smile on her face.

"Isn't she a sweetheart?"

"I think that's an understatement."

"Caitlin said I should surprise you."

"You did."

"Caitlin called Chloe her miracle baby. She was really low after you went home. She was scheduled to start radiation treatment in a few weeks, so she went to the doctor's office to complete the necessary paperwork. She told me when she was filling out the forms, she stopped and stared at one of the questions. It read, *Are you pregnant?* Caitlin walked up to the desk and asked the woman who had given her the form, 'What if I am unsure about being pregnant?' The nurse said, 'I think we should find out.' A few hours later, she came home with a big smile on her face and announced she was pregnant. I just looked at her and started crying. Caitlin told me I should stop crying because she was going to be fine and the baby was too. Three months later, she had surgery, and five months after that, Chloe was born."

"That was a miracle."

"The miracle was the past fifteen years we had with Caitlin and Chloe. Caitlin told Colin and me that she was going to have her baby and fill the child's life with love, and that's exactly what she did."

"From what I just witnessed, I think she did a great job. How long has Chloe been taking piano lessons?"

"Since she was five. Ryan got her one of those toy pianos as a Christmas present when she was about four, and it was soon the only toy she would play with. She was so cute. She would use her stuffed animals and dolls as her audience. She would place them in rows and then tell them to be quiet and pay attention while she played for them."

"That is cute."

"The strange thing was that some of the music she played sounded good, at least to us. So Ryan suggested she start taking lessons, and then he found a teacher who was willing to take her as a student. She was over a year younger than any other student."

"How did she do?"

"Great, and now she is studying under a professor at university on Saturdays. She wants to study music when she goes to uni."

"I'm sure you are proud of her."

"We are."

As I looked at Kathleen, the love she had for Chloe was obvious. I looked back at the garden. "I never knew this was here. It's beautiful."

"It wasn't the last time you were here, Michael."

"Oh."

"Chloe saw a movie when she was six years old, and when she came over, she asked if we could have a garden like the one in the movie. In a little more than a month, Colin, Ryan, and Caitlin had created one. She thinks of it as her sanctuary. Chloe often curled up on that bench with her head in Caitlin's lap as her mum read to her. I believe this will always be a special place for Chloe. She…" Kathleen stopped, took a deep breath, and smiled.

I could tell any reminder of the loss of Caitlin was still difficult. "Kathleen, I'm sure it will always be special to Chloe. It is amazing, and I think all

those times she shared here with her mom will only
serve to make it more special to Chloe."

"Thank you, Michael. As I said earlier, I still
have my moments."

"That's understandable."

"Would you like to go back inside and have
some more coffee?"

"Sure."

As we walked back toward the house, I stopped.
"What is that called?" I asked as I pointed at the
shrubs that served as the outside border.

"That is called heather, and you will see a lot of it
later. It grows wild in the countryside, and when you go
to see Caitlin, you'll see it in its natural element. Now
that purple flower to your left in the central bed—"

"The one with the thorns…"

"Yes. It is the thistle, the national flower, and
there are some interesting stories about how that
came to be. I'll let Colin tell you those. He enjoys
telling people about the history of our people."

"Okay."

A light mist started falling, and Kathleen looked
up at the sky. "Let's get inside before it starts raining."

Chapter Thirty-Four

Colin picked me up at the hotel at 1:00 p.m. Kathleen was disappointed that I didn't stay for lunch, but I told her I really needed some time to process my surprise. I assured her all was fine, and she reluctantly agreed. I was still in a state of shock and thought an hour or so alone would give me a chance to think about what I was going to do and to look at my gifts from Chloe and Caitlin. I had just finished looking at the album chronicling Chloe's life when Colin called to tell me he would be at the hotel in fifteen minutes. It had only been a cursory look, and I knew I would take the time later to savor the special moments of this exceptional young lady—my newly discovered daughter.

Colin warned me to dress for cold, damp weather, and I was glad he did. The wind had picked up, and a light mist peppered the windshield as we drove out of Edinburgh. I wanted to talk with Colin about Ryan and Chloe, but he was more interested in pointing out obscure places that were sites of his fishing exploits or, on occasion, some landmark that pertained to clan history. I soon decided it would be best to let him talk for now, and when we started back, I would try to bring up a matter I had been thinking about. It occurred to me, while I was looking at the album, Chloe and Ryan were my children and were entitled to share in their father's success.

"Michael, lad, you have to fish the Firth of Forth."

"I may try to come back soon if I can work it out. Maybe we could go fishing then."

"You would love it, and the fish, I caught some as long as your arm!"

"You sound like a cousin of mine." I glanced at my watch and noted we had been driving for thirty minutes when Colin turned off the road onto a narrow lane, which led back to a church in the distance. Colin slowed as we entered the cemetery, and I could tell by the condition of some of the markers that they were incredibly old.

"Does the church still have services?"

"Yes. I'm not sure how often, but Caitlin and Chloe came when they were able."

Colin stopped the car. "Michael, I'll let you have some time alone with Caitlin. I'm going to see if an old mate of mine is home, and I'll come back in thirty minutes or so. I want—"

I interrupted, "Colin, I have never been here. I have no idea where the grave is located."

"Yes, I was going to tell you to go around to the back of the church and look for the tallest marker. It belongs to her mum's clan, the Douglas's. When you get close to the marker, I'm sure you will be able to find her grave. Though there is no gravestone yet, it will be easy to tell which is our Caitlin's."

"Okay. I was just a little concerned about how long it might take to find her grave. Thanks, Colin," I said as I got out of the car.

"See you in a wee bit, Michael."

"Okay."

I watched as he drove out of the cemetery. I wondered why he didn't want to go with me, but in a way, I was glad. It would be just Caitie and me. I knew Colin didn't hate me, though he had ample reasons to do so. However, if there had been any dispute about contacting me when Caitie died, I was sure Kathleen and Chloe were the deciding factors.

I walked around the church and saw the marker Colin referred to earlier. Thankfully, the rain stopped, but the grass was wet. So I crouched on one knee beside Caitie's grave. As I looked across the landscape, I could see why she chose this place. The small hills surrounding the church were adorned with wildflowers and heather as in the garden. It was nature's celebration of life. I could hear Caitie saying to me, "Michael, this is the Scotland I love. This is where I belong, my home."

I put my hand on the wet earth that covered the grave and thought of how unfair life had been to us in so many ways. "Caitie, I wish I had known. I'm sure you had your reasons, but I would have given anything to hold you in my arms one more time. I love you, Caitie, and I missed you so these past fifteen years. Christy and the kids made it easier, but you were always in my thoughts. I know it was the right thing to do, but not seeing or talking with you was so hard at times. You were the better person, Caitie, and your strength made it possible for us both to have a life without hurting so many of the people we love.

"Ten days. Caitie, can you believe we only had ten days together? I know I shouldn't complain. At least we did finally discover the truth. I often think about how different our lives would have been if I hadn't found that letter. We would have never known what we experienced when we were so young was real, and there would be no Chloe. By the way, Caitie, I am a little old for that kind of surprise. She is so sweet. I thought you might like to know I intend to be a part of her life if she will allow it.

I am going to talk with Christy, Mom, and Becky when I return home. She is innocent in all this and should be acknowledged by the Williams family as my daughter. Thank you for telling her about me and assuring her that her father loves her. I do."

I took the silk magnolia out of the box I brought with me and placed it on the grave. "Caitie, I remember how you fell in love with the magnolias at Twin Oaks, so I wanted to bring you one. I love you, Caitie."

There was an artist in Roseville who made the silk magnolia. I had asked her if she could fashion something underneath the flower that would keep it in place. She had added a flat solid base that was hidden by the flower to serve the purpose. As I stood and looked down at the magnolia blossom, it looked as though someone came to visit and dropped a beautiful flower on the grave of one they loved.

For a few minutes, I marveled at the beauty of this place Caitie had chosen. As my eyes settled on the old church with its simple design, I started to appreciate its beauty. The rough-hewn irregular-shaped stones used in its construction hearkened to a distant millennium. The men who built this church were true artisans. As I continued to stare at the church, I could almost feel the rough, granular texture of the stone wall facing this part of the cemetery. I was reminded of a time when I noticed my grandmother staring at a painting her husband had given her of an old wooden church. When I asked her what she found so fascinating about the painting, she said, "One day, you will understand, Michael. It's about one's life experience. When I look at that painting, I don't just see the church. I am in the church I attended as a child, sitting beside my sister, singing hymns. For a few moments, I am there." I am beginning to understand. Love you, Gran.

I bent and touched the wet earth again. "Goodbye for now, my love." I slowly retraced my steps, and as I walked around the church, I saw Colin waiting for me.

As I took a seat in the car, I confirmed a suspicion. Colin had enjoyed a drink or two with his friend. "Did you enjoy the visit with your mate?"

"Yes, we had a pint and talked about when we were young lads."

"Sounds good."

"Yes, it was good to see him. It has been a while."

I thought it was time to raise the topic concerning Ryan and Chloe before Colin started talking about something else. I feared the drinking would most likely make him even more talkative, and I had experienced earlier how much he liked a captive audience. I knew it might have been easier to have approached Kathleen with the matter, but I felt Colin would have been offended since I was certain he thought, as head of the family, it was his approval that should be secured in such affairs. "Colin, I need to talk with you about a matter, and I don't want you to be offended." I paused to allow him a chance to respond, and for a moment, I wondered if he had heard the question.

He finally glanced over at me and said, "And why might I be offended?"

"Because you are a proud man, and there is nothing wrong with that. You have a great deal to be proud of."

"What is this about, Michael?"

"Colin, I have been very fortunate in life, and if Caitlin and I were married, she and her children would have benefitted from my success."

"We are doing fine, Michael."

I could sense the pride and suppressed anger in his voice, and I knew I had to be careful not to offend him. "I know that, Colin, but do you think I loved your daughter?"

"Aye, you would have been daft not to love her."

"Colin, had I not been married when I found out about Ryan, I would have married Caitlin, and we would not be having this conversation. I am asking you to allow me to give my children what is rightfully theirs. I would never want to insult you nor would I ever question the role you played in helping my children grow into such great young people. I will always be grateful for what you and Kathleen have done for Caitlin and me. I am merely asking your permission to give my children what they are entitled to."

"How can you? Caitlin wouldn't want Ryan to find out."

"Yes, I know, and I think there is a way to comply with her wishes if you will agree to it. Please keep in mind, Colin, I am merely asking for your help in giving our children and your grandchildren what should rightfully be theirs. I know you take great pride in being a member of a clan, and though I am not familiar with clan law, I would hope it would let a father give his son and daughter an inheritance. Would clan law deny this, Colin?" As I finished, I saw a slight smile appear on Colin's face, and my hope was that it was a sign that I might have won the battle.

"I think clan law would allow it, so I'll agree. And if you are interested, I can get you a copy of some early clan law."

"That would be nice," I said, thinking it might make a good gift for Tom. I also hoped my appearance of an interest in such would further cement Colin's approval.

Chapter Thirty-Five

I t was 3:00 p.m. when we turned onto the street where Colin lived, and I saw a car parked in front of the house.

"Sophie must have dropped by. You must meet her Michael. She's Ryan's wife."

"Yes, I'd like that."

As we walked in, Colin turned and went into the living room where Chloe, Kathleen, and a young lady I assumed was Sophie were sitting. *That's odd*, I thought, for it was the first time I could remember not going straight through to the kitchen.

Colin leaned over, hugged the young lady, and then turned back to me. "Sophie, this is Michael Williams."

"It's nice to meet you, Michael. Caitlin and Ryan have often spoken of you."

Sophie then stood, and I almost congratulated her but decided it might be best to say nothing. I had made that mistake before, and it was a difficult one to walk back.

"Well, I hate to do this, but I need to get to the pub," Sophie said as she smiled at me. "I guess I will see all of you there in a bit. We can talk then, and you can see Ryan, Mr. Williams. He is looking forward to seeing you again."

"I'm not—"

Colin interrupted, "Sorry, Michael, I know I should have said something earlier, but Ryan wanted you to eat at the pub before you leave so he would have a chance to see you."

"That's fine. I just can't miss my flight. I need to be at the airport no later than six."

"We'll make sure you get there, Michael."

"Okay." However, I wasn't so sure, but I knew I was going to have to trust Colin because I didn't think I could refuse with Chloe smiling at me.

"Then I guess I'll see you in a few minutes," Sophie said. She then hugged Colin again, shook hands with me, and left.

For an awkward moment, we all stood there, and then Kathleen said, "Colin, let's give Chloe and Michael a chance to talk. I need to freshen up before we go." Colin nodded, and they went up the stairs that were just outside the room. Chloe and I were now alone.

"Let's sit at the piano," Chloe suggested.

"Sure." I had not realized there was a piano in the room. The last time I sat in this room was the last time I saw Caitie, and I believed a recliner was in the place now occupied by the piano. It was what they call an upright, and there was a bench that was slid away from the piano. Chloe sat down and motioned for me to sit beside her.

"It came to me when I was at my lesson that you have never heard me play, so I thought if you don't mind—"

"Chloe, I'd be honored to hear you play."

She just sat there for a minute. I started to think she must have changed her mind, then she began. With a single delicate finger, she lightly tapped one key. At first, the tempo was very slow, and the note was barely perceptible. It gradually grew in volume and tempo to the point where it was easily heard. This went on until I considered asking Chloe if she wanted to do this later, but I stopped. There was no later. Then she started to move her hands across the keyboard. It was almost like a child exploring the instrument, yet it was musical. Then it changed again. Chloe was now playing in a way that caused me to stare at her in wonder. How could a child—our child—play so beautifully? And then she went back to the single key, slowly dropping the volume and tempo until she let her finger rest on the key, and it was silent.

I saw the tears in Chloe's eyes as she took a small tissue from her pocket and wiped them. "That was beautiful, Chloe."

"Mom said you played."

"Yes, but not like that."

"Thank you, Dad. It's called *A Tribute to Caitlin*."

I now understood. The single key, it was Caitie's heartbeat.

"It's actually much longer, but I knew you wouldn't have the time to listen to the entire piece. That's why I took so long to start. I had to decide how to condense the composition and yet allow you a chance to listen to each part of her life."

I suddenly realized there were no sheets of music on the stand. Chloe had done all this in her head. "It was beautiful, and I'm sure your mom would have loved it."

"I made you a copy of the entire piece. I thought it might be nice to let my grandmother watch it as well. I hope she will be pleased."

"Chloe, I think she will be amazed."

"Thank you."

"What does your instructor think about the piece?"

"He thought it was very good."

"Is that what he said?"

"He said it showed real promise, but I hate it when people brag about themselves. This is the copy I made you," Chloe said as she took a thumb drive from the top of the piano and gave it to me.

"Chloe, I think your talent speaks for itself, and thank you for making the video. I will enjoy watching it."

"You're welcome."

"Chloe, I will either be back to see you soon or work it out where you can visit me during a break. Also, before I leave today, I need the web address of your school so I can look at the school calendar and make some plans."

"Okay, and I wanted to ask if you would continue writing me. I love reading about your life."

"I would enjoy that, Chloe. I'll make it a little more frequently if that's okay with you."

"That would be nice, and would it be okay if I write to you, Dad?"

"Yes, I would like that very much, Chloe. I look forward to getting to know more about you and your life here." I was gradually acclimating to hearing Chloe refer to me as her dad, and it was a pleasant adjustment. Footsteps coming from the stairway reminded me that the time I had remaining in Scotland was growing short, and it was time to go to the pub.

"Michael, did you need to go by the hotel?" Colin asked as he came into view.

"Yes, I need to grab my bag and check out. It will only take a few minutes, and then I can leave for the airport from the pub."

"Okay, we better get started then."

Chapter Thirty-Six

I glanced at my watch and saw it was 4:25 p.m. as we drove out of the hotel parking lot. We had dropped Kathleen and Chloe off at the pub and then went to the hotel. Everything was going remarkably smooth since my arrival in Scotland, and I guess that was why I was concerned. I felt if I could just make it to the airport and get on the plane, all would be fine. I considered telling Colin I was just going to talk with Ryan for a few minutes and then take a taxi out to the airport, but I knew that wouldn't please him. So I said nothing. I knew I was tempting fate, but it was worth the slight risk to spend some time with Chloe and Ryan.

"I told Kathleen about our talk earlier, and she thought it was nice of you to consider Ryan and Chloe…"

He paused, and I hoped it wasn't for the reason I feared. "Is she okay with what I suggested?"

"Yes, I…"

I didn't listen to the rest. The important thing was, I was being allowed to make our children's lives better, and then we pulled up to the pub.

As we walked in, I could see there was a good-sized crowd. Colin went over to help Ryan at the bar, and I went in the direction of several waving hands Colin had pointed out. When I arrived at the table, I got a surprise. Erin, Caitlin's close friend, was sitting at the table with Kathleen, Sophie, and Chloe. "I'm not so sure I should sit at this table."

"You don't have much of a choice unless you choose to sit at the bar, and I'm not so sure they'll welcome a yank. We promise not to bite," Kathleen said as she laughed then continued as she looked at Erin, "or slap you."

"I have to admit I've had some personal experience with a certain fiery Scottish woman, and I have no desire to repeat it."

At this, Erin choked momentarily on her drink and started laughing. "That was memorable. I can see your face even now," Erin managed through the laughter.

Chloe laughed and added, "Auntie Erin was just telling us about your last encounter with her, Dad."

Ryan was suddenly beside me. "It's good to see you, Mr. Williams. I just wish it was under different circumstances."

"Yes, your sister was a special person, Ryan."

"I appreciate that. Thank you for coming. My sister cared a great deal for you."

"And I for her."

"Has Sophie told you the good news?"

"No," I said as I looked over at Sophie, who blushed.

"There will be a new Campbell added to the clan roles in about five months."

"That is great news. Congratulations, Ryan."

"Thank you, sir. I understand you are on a tight schedule. So all I need is your order, and we'll have it out in a few minutes. A well-kept secret among the locals is that the best food in town is served in the pubs."

"Yes, someone told me that the last time I was in Edinburgh."

"Caitlin told me about your experience with haggis. So if I could make a suggestion."

"Sure."

"The fish-and-chips. The fish is fresh today, and the cod is really good."

"That sounds great."

"You won't be disappointed."

For the next hour, I ate a good meal and shared the time with a group of people who dearly loved Caitie. When Colin came over and told me it was time to leave, I gave each of them a hug. I then told Chloe she would hear from me soon. When she whispered, "Love you, Dad" in my ear, I kissed her on the cheek and told her I loved her too.

Traffic was light, and I arrived at the airport a few minutes after six. Erin said I would make my flight if I got there before six twenty, and she was right. I talked to Christy and Tom while waiting to board the plane, so all I had to do was wait—wait until I flew out of Scotland. Strange. Nine hours earlier, I thought, when I left Scotland, it would be the closing of a chapter in my life. Now my hope was it was the beginning of a wonderful new chapter—Chloe.

Epilogue

Two months later

I have found solace in solitude, for when I am alone, Caitie still comes to me. I first noticed this while standing in the cemetery in Scotland when I visited her grave. She came to me as a barely audible whisper, a repeated echo. "I love you, Michael. I love you…" I always respond, "I love you, Caitie" as I did that day, and invariably a smile fills my face as I recall how fortunate I was to have loved and been loved by Caitie.

I have started running since I returned to Roseville. Christy has tried for years to get me to join her in the gym. On occasion, I do, but I prefer the open air. She is pleased, and I found the runs comforting. My favorite run is one that takes me through Twin Oaks, and I often stop in the shade of those massive two oaks that frame the entrance where Caitie and I stood over thirty years ago and shared our dreams. I stop, and I listen until, once again, I hear that whisper echoing, "I love you, Michael. I love you…"

About the Author

Author Darrell Denham is a retired teacher who married his childhood sweetheart. He enjoys spending time with his family and vacationing on the Emerald Coast of Florida. He currently resides in Tifton, Georgia. You may follow him at Darrell Denham on Facebook where he has links to his web page and other social media platforms.